Caught

in the

Crossfire

G·K
Hall
&C°.

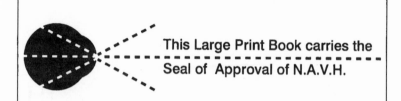

This Large Print Book carries the
Seal of Approval of N.A.V.H.

Caught

in the

Crossfire

The trials and triumphs
of African believers
through an era of tribulation

LEVI KEIDEL

G.K. Hall & Co. • Thorndike, Maine

Published in 2000 by arrangement with Herald Press, a division of Mennonite Publishing House, Inc.

G.K. Hall Large Print Inspirational Series.

The text of this Large Print edition is unabridged.
Other aspects of the book may vary from the original edition.

Set in 16 pt. Plantin by Elena Picard.

Printed in the United States on permanent paper.

Library of Congress Cataloging-in-Publication Data

Keidel, Levi O.
    Caught in the crossfire : the trials and triumphs of African
believers through an era of tribulation / Levi Keidel.
      p. cm.
    Originally published: Scottdale, Pa. : Herald Press, 1979
    ISBN 0-7838-9008-7 (lg. print : hc : alk. paper)
    1. Congo (Democratic Republic) — History — Civil War,
1960–1965 — Fiction. 2. Mennonites — Missions — Fiction.
3. Missions — Fiction. I. Title.
PS3561.E375 C38 2000
813′.54—dc21
                                              00-023515

Dedicated to today's African Christians
whose faith is being painfully forged
by the fires of tribulation.

Author's Preface

My wife and I have completed four terms of missionary service to Zaire, Central Africa. Each time we return to North America we encounter a higher level of material affluence. Each time we return, we are startled to observe how affluence has been mobilized to remove every form of discomfort from human experience. Plush furnishings, labor-saving appliances, and patent medicines which promise relief to our myriad physical ailments all serve to subtly convince us that suffering is not only unnecessary; it is purposeless and even wrong.

Leaders of Christian opinion dutifully respond to the caress of these creature comforts: musicians compose syncopated joy-joy lyrics which tell us that believing in Jesus will dispel all of our troubles, preachers purport that God is a benign grandparent who only owes us endless benevolences, and theologians argue that tribulation could never befall the church during this dispensation. If perchance Christians should encounter the threat of suffering, the patent-medicine complex applies: the Bible has a full range of neatly labeled remedies to deal with it.

While living in Zaire we experienced two revolutions. We report firsthand that the church today DOES endure tribulation, and that such an experience DOES serve a purpose in the providence of God. Beginning in January of 1964 a communist-oriented insurrection thrust people of Zaire into a long night of suffering. What happens when a Christian community is suddenly caught in a carefully woven net of organized violence? How do believers cope with it? What do they learn from such an experience? In Kwilu Province, which is the geographic focus of this book, three Christian leaders felt compelled to take differing positions toward the uprising and reaped vastly differing fortunes.

This story is a true account of actual persons and events. I have used a minimum of fictionalizing to enhance the dramatic potential of the story and to honor the request that its Zairian sources remain anonymous.

Levi Keidel

Chapter One

Three and one-half years had passed since Congo, now known as Zaire, had gained political independence. People living in that vast land which sprawls across the waistline of Africa would never forget their first Independence Day. Its atmosphere had been heady, exhilarating. A sovereign nation was born. Fourteen million people, freed from irksome colonial rule, suddenly discovered power to shape their own destinies. Ambitious visionary black leaders took their places at the helm of government.

But subsequent events soon vaporized the effervescence of that historic day. Leaders, little trained in the science of government, fell heir to power and wealth beyond their ability to wisely manage. With the passing of months, white colonial prejudice was replaced by tribal prejudice. Then came increasing social disintegration, the inevitable result of abused power and of misused public funds.

The common people suffered the most. During forty years of colonial rule they had been voiceless. Racial discrimination had separated them from the possibility of self-rule. Now that separation had grown to a yawning chasm. People simmered in their powerlessness, their discontent, their disillusionment, their feelings of animosity toward faithless leaders whose indifference progressively worsened their lot.

Congo's rough-and-tumble politics left a continuing residue of dissident leaders ousted from the mainstream of national life. Having received little political training from their colonial predecessors, they sought it elsewhere. Among them was Pierre Mulele.

Mulele, articulate and intelligent, was expelled from a Catholic high school at age 15 for refusing to believe in the virgin birth of Christ. He served in the colonial-era army, deserted it, and eventually secured a low-echelon job in the colonial government. He served in Congo's first national government under Prime Minister Lumumba as Minister of Education. That lasted for two months, when Lumumba was ousted from power. Then, Mulele's previous contacts with representatives from Eastern countries led him to China where he studied for a year and a half.

He had just returned last dry season. He settled in his home area in the rural hinterland of Kwilu Province in east central Zaire. There he roamed through the villages, nursed the disenchantments of the people, promised to redress their wrongs, and won widespread support. He conscripted masses of idle young men into an army, taught them tactics of guerrilla warfare, and focused their hate on the leaders and organizations of the incumbent national government.

It was early 1964. At night unorganized bands of young insurrectionists called the *jeunesse* (French for "youth") roamed the countryside. Armed with bows, arrows, spears, and wide-bladed two-foot-long machetes, they were bent on destroying centers of authority in the name of Mulele. Outbreaks of violence were scattered at first, then became more frequent. Now, in Kwilu Province, trouble spots like pustules on a pain-wracked body were erupting everywhere.

These events occupied the mind of Pastor Paul Lamba on this particular Tuesday evening. He was a heavy paunchy middle-aged man of medium stature. Converted to Christ when a youth, he had finished primary school and a two-year Bible course here on the mission station of Kende. Ever since then he had worked for the mission. He was married, the father of a nine-year-old daughter and a six-year-old son. His long years of faithfulness had earned him unparalleled respect among those who knew him. Now, he was senior pastor on the station and the spiritual leader of Christians in villages surrounding it.

He sat eating at a worn wooden table in his home. A kerosene lamp before him lit the simple square room with a dim orange glow. Exit doors stood open on two of the room's opposite sides. Its four whitewashed walls were decorated with a

11

few religious mottoes, a large picture frame displaying an assortment of faded photographs, and a calendar.

Ordinarily Pastor Lamba enjoyed eating. This evening was different. Anxiety about these tempestuous events had dulled his appetite. It had tied his middle like a wasp's. He had a premonition of impending trouble — even of calamity. He had tried to dismiss it half-a-dozen times, but each time it stubbornly returned. Leaving a loaf of cassava mush and a bowl of greens half finished, he pushed his rotund body away from the table. He got up, went to an aluminum washbasin on a stand in the corner, and washed his hands.

"Pastor." His wife had entered the back door which opened toward the kitchen hut. "Ilunga has come. He wants to talk with you."

"Tell him to come in."

She picked up the supper dishes, swiped off the scarred tabletop with a hand, shifted the lamp to its center, and left. A young man of medium height and slight muscular build entered.

"Greetings, Ilunga. Sit down." The pastor gestured with his nose toward a table chair as he finished wiping his hands on a towel. James Ilunga had been born and raised in the area. Last year he had finished upper-level theological training and returned home. He was married, with six small children. Recently ordained, he was the second pastor on Kende mission station. Enthusiastic and aggressive, he taught in the local

12

Bible Institute. Tonight his face registered consternation. He pulled a chair away from the table and sat down.

"Pastor Paul," he spoke in a subdued voice, "these days the elephant grass has ears. May we close the doors?"

Paul Lamba closed the two outside doors, drew a chair close to his visitor and sat down.

"I rejoice for your coming," he said. "What is the news?"

"Father," Ilunga addressed him respectfully, "I must ask you this question. What is your thinking about the events which are happening around us these days?"

"Do you mean the things the jeunesse are doing?"

"Yes."

The elder pastor paused, frowned, looked down at hands clasped around his ample midriff, then lifted his eyes and responded with hesitation.

"For all of these days I have been simply leaving these things in the hands of God. I have been telling myself that these affairs will not reach us here. People on a mission station have work in their hands to do. They have schools where they can study. Why should they join those who are revolting against the government?"

Lamba watched Ilunga's face darken with a frown. Did he catch in it a flicker of disdain? The young man continued.

13

"People know in their hearts why they decide to support the revolution. Perhaps some people here have already joined it; others have not. You see for yourself how the movement has become strong and spread like a dry prairie fire. These affairs began only three months ago. First, we heard news that far away the cable of a big ferry was cut. Then bridges were destroyed. The palm oil factory was burned down. Trucks loaded with soldiers armed with guns fell into pits; rebels attacked the soldiers and killed them with machetes! Then we began hearing that state posts were attacked at night and burned. Government workers at those places were caught and chopped to pieces, or beaten to death. I heard Kinshasa radio say that 120 of them have been killed. Then last week school buildings were burned not far from here. Three days ago the cable at the ferry crossing down the road from us was cut; the ferry floated downstream. Last night they burned down the buildings of our local government post. Didn't you see with your own eyes the houses burning in the valley? Father, it is always good to put things into the hands of God. But lifting your foot is one thing, climbing the ladder is another. You should recognize that these affairs have already reached us. Can you keep the smell of smoke from entering your hut by closing the door?"

Pastor Lamba wrinkled his forehead in concentration. He was Ilunga's senior by perhaps fifteen years. Since Ilunga had returned from

14

theological school, he always seemed so aggressive, so pretentious. The older man found it threatening. Was James Ilunga suggesting that Lamba's lack of understanding of the present situation indicated he was not measuring up to the responsibilities of his leadership role? Or had James really come with honest motives, wanting to help? If the crisis continued to mount, what could they do?

"Is there no way of stopping these jeunesse?" Lamba muttered half to himself.

"Government soldiers have not been able to stop them," the young pastor continued. "This has given them courage. They teach things which confuse the thinking of people. They say that any one of their arrows has the power of eight gun cartridges. They say that when soldiers shoot at them, they shout words which change bullets to water. They can change themselves into palm trees so that no one can recognize them. Mulele has power to send them messages wherever they are. At night they travel swiftly and silently, like birds. People seeing the amazing things the guerrillas have done, without being hindered, are believing these stories. For what reason will the rebels be stopped? The elders say, 'The wise hunter may challenge a lion, but never a lightning bolt.' If the army with its guns cannot stop them, only a foolish person would raise his finger to resist them."

Ilunga paused. His face showed increasing stress. He looked intently at the elder man as if mustering courage; finally he spoke.

"Pastor, I have come here not for my sake, but for yours. It is useless to think about stopping the jeunesse. The person who tries to restrain them will be crushed like a butterfly beneath a tumbling boulder. The rebels are about to arrive. If you want to escape with your life, you should now be thinking about how you are going to receive them."

Lamba did not want to believe his ears.

"What are you saying?" he asked. "Why should they want to do me harm?"

"The rebels always search out those people in the village who have bad hearts — those who have grudges to avenge. You have helped expel some students from school. You have excommunicated backsliders from church. Be sure that the jeunesse have gathered such people to themselves. They have covenanted to even scores with you. Our forefathers said, 'Wildcat, don't be amused that the hunter is chasing other animals; he is also chasing you'. Together the rebels see you as a stumbling block to their revolution. When they attack, they fear nothing. They do whatever they want. My father, don't you hear what I'm saying?"

Lamba was hearing. The words settled like rocks in the pit of his stomach.

"It would be good for you to decide what to do for your own sake. Then, we two pastors could agree on what needs to be done to help the missionaries."

16

The thought of harming the missionaries was alarming. Five missionaries now lived on Kende station because he had urged them to come. Traditionally, people had the highest regard for the missionaries.

"Do you think they have it in mind to harm the missionary?" Paul asked incredulously.

"Only God knows what the rebels are thinking," Ilunga replied. "They do not have good hearts toward persons they feel have hoarded wealth. The missionaries have cars and nice homes. They brought the Book of God which teaches that violence is wrong. We hear that Mulele wants to drive out all the white people. Then on top of this, villagers are upset about what happened today."

"Explain to me."

"That the missionary leader . . . when he left this morning . . . he had with him in the car the local government administrator who was ill. They were going to Mwangu, where there is a hospital. Everybody knows that Mwangu is a government center where there are many soldiers. Then this afternoon three truckloads of soldiers came. You saw them. They tormented a few people, seized animals from the villagers, and left. Now people are whispering that the missionaries collaborate with the national government; the one this morning called the soldiers. This incident has enflamed the anger of the jeunesse. As they see it, why should they love the missionaries?"

Lamba's supper was not setting good. He felt nausea.

"What is your wisdom for pacifying the anger of the rebels toward us?" he asked.

"When a wise man knows a big storm is coming, he will prepare for it. He will replace rotten wall sticks with strong ones. He will tie his hut roof down securely. By doing this, he may withstand the terror of the storm and survive. If he does not, he may perish. Now the guerrillas see you as their enemy. If you send them word that you have changed your heart and will receive them, you may withstand the terror of this storm and survive. Also, then together we may weaken their anger toward the missionaries."

Pastor Lamba weighed his options. He was still annoyed by the young man's pretentiousness. Did James know what he was talking about? If so, what were his sources of information? If not, could he create so convincing a story purely for the purpose of pre-empting Lamba's position? If the senior pastor rejected the young man's counsel, and later events proved this foreboding picture to be correct, James would be first to declare before the people, "I told him so." But more seriously, Lamba might well lose his life; and his inaction would mean greater jeopardy to the missionaries. On the other hand, if he followed James' advice and made conciliatory gestures toward the rebels whose conduct revolted him, how could he live with his conscience? And later when army troops succeeded in quelling the rebellion, what price would they exact from him, a leader of the people who had collaborated with the enemy? Carefully he framed his response.

"James, I want to thank you for coming tonight. Your words have much weight. All the Christians here look to me as their shepherd. Even the missionaries come to me for counsel. I need some time to think about these things. I will give you my answer later."

The visitor stood up.

"Think it over well," he said with resignation. "But don't take too long." He turned to leave.

"Tell me," Lamba added as an afterthought. "Do you think they might attack the mission station?"

"I have no way of knowing the truth," he replied. "I did not want to mention it. But I heard a whisper that they are coming to burn it down tonight."

He turned and slipped out of the door into the darkness.

Pastor Paul Lamba gaped after his visitor unbelievingly. He sensed an overwhelming weakness. He moved back to his table chair and dropped himself onto it. Was this the reason for his ominous premonition? He must do something. He had to tell the missionaries. Yes, that was what he must do. If these things really happened, and he had not warned them, how could he forgive himself? First, he must leave word with his wife. He found her in the kitchen hut, sitting with his two children by the coals of the supper fire.

"Tembo, Pastor James says things are very bad. I'm going to talk with the missionaries."

He did not wait for her response. He strode rapidly some fifty yards to the home of the Jim Bertsche family, senior missionaries on Kende station. His eye caught a glimpse of them through a front window. They were seated in a circle praying. He did not want to disturb them. Then he realized that since Ilunga had told him of these troubling matters, he had not prayed. Why had he come here without first praying? He had made a mistake. He would go home and pray. Maybe that would give him some new perspective on these problems. Then later he would return and talk with the missionaries.

Quietly he turned and left to carry out his plan. To go pray, yes. To return, no. There would not be time.

Chapter Two

Jim Bertsche completed evening prayers with his wife and eight-year-old son Tim, and kissed the boy good night. It was too early for Bertsche to retire. He felt the need to reduce the clutter of accumulated business on his office desk. He would go work for a while.

He went into an adjacent room which served as his office, settled his stocky frame onto a wooden chair, and pulled himself to the desk. Where should he start? Should he try to sort out business affairs still tangled from their voyage to Africa four months ago? Should he deal with matters of rejuvenating a mission station unoccupied by the missionaries since post-independence disturbances 2½ years ago? Should he edit a few pages of Scripture translation? He adjusted his heavy glasses, drew his fingers through thick graying hair, and fidgeted with indecision. He might as well admit it. He could not give himself to any of these things. His mind was distracted by the portentous events of these days.

Three months ago when he and fellow missionaries first heard the faint rumblings of an insurgent youth movement headed by a certain Pierre Mulele two hundred miles away, they gave the rumors only passing interest. But the movement had spread so rapidly and so threatened the structures of ordered society that it now demanded the center of the missionaries' attention.

For weeks Bertsche had known that youth were slipping out of the village periodically for undisclosed destinations and for varying periods of time. But local chiefs and church leaders continued to affirm that the jeunesse were not around. This claim was no longer true. Each morning people were buffeted by a fresh set of rumors: buildings at a nearby school post were burned, the teachers manhandled; a village chief had been threatened with death unless he pledged allegiance to the movement; a local government authority and his aides, outspoken opponents of the revolution, were killed, their families burned to death in his house. Stories ran rampant. To separate fact from fiction was impossible. But one thing was now clear: the population's sympathies were with the rebels; and rule in the area was effectively shifting from the national government to the insurrectionists.

This was Tuesday. Bertsche had been at a distant church administrative meeting last week. On Friday he and Stephen Kimeya, a leading layman from Mudidi station, had received radio messages informing them of deteriorating conditions and urging that they return home immediately. On Saturday, the day Jim arrived back at Kende, a truckload of government soldiers came on an inspection tour. Moments after their departure, the local ferry was mysteriously disabled. This cut off any further direct travel by road to or from the east.

Because of these events, an ominous fear descended on the mission compound. Jim recounted the signs of mounting tension. He did not hear the happy noises of schoolchildren playing at recess any more . . . nor the good-natured banter between the Congolese cook and village women gathered at the back door selling produce. Instead parents kept children at home. Women feared going to their fields. Adults, their faces drawn with apprehension, clustered to exchange the latest rumors and then drifted their separate ways. Increasing numbers of people dropped by missionary residences to share their fears. A few had slept in the missionaries' homes, they were "afraid of the soldiers."

People took precautions to protect their personal effects. Some brought things to store in the missionaries' houses, hoping they would be safe there. Others packed clothing and dishes into metal trunks and buried them in secret hiding places. Others, carrying everything they could on bicycles and in bundles on their heads, had decided to return on foot to their home villages.

The movement was a clandestine operation. A government building would mysteriously catch

23

fire at night; and when authorities interrogated people the next day, no one had a clue as to what had happened. In this manner, the revolution, like an elusive phantom, would suddenly appear and then vanish again.

However, in spite of these things, Bertsche had reasons for hope. Up to now these attacks had been directed primarily toward the incumbent government. There had been no move against mission stations. It was rumored that rebels had surrounded Kende station last night, but their Protestant leader had dissuaded them from causing any disturbance. These facts encouraged him to believe that widespread respect and appreciation for the work of the mission discouraged insurrectionists from bothering them. Hopefully the mission would remain uninvolved and be allowed to carry on its work.

Bertsche and his wife had sought to follow the leading of the Lord when they returned to the field to reoccupy this station. A primary purpose of their return had been to reopen the Bible Institute which trained pastors for the entire mission area. Political and tribal disorders had plagued its operation elsewhere. It had been transferred to Kende station, to what was felt a more neutral area. An entire complex of new buildings had been constructed for it. Harold and Gladys Graber and their five children had fled as refugees from a war-torn area 3½ years ago. They re-outfitted themselves and had just returned to the field. Harold and Gladys, with their five-year-old daughter, Jeanette, had taken up residence at Kende to direct activities of the Institute.

Bertsche himself hoped to make substantial progress toward completing the monumental task of translating the Old Testament into the local vernacular; his veteran assistant in translation work, David Kalau, had relocated with his wife and six children here at Kende to resume work. Bertsche, his family, the Grabers, and Selma Unruh, a single lady, had returned to live at Kende station because they shared a vision. Surely God would vindicate their faith by fulfilling it.

The Bible Institute students were married and many of them had small children. Most of them came from mission station areas to the east, beyond the Loange River. With their wives and children, they numbered over fifty. Current events caused them much stress. Students had wanted to suspend studies so that they and their families might return to their less-troubled home areas. Now that the ferry was out, the Loange River was a three-day foot journey away. The field chairman of the missionary personnel had visited Kende station this morning. The missionaries together with him had agreed that any disruption of normal activities would only add to the unrest. They must exercise faith that God held all things in His control. Bible Institute classes would continue. Students reluctantly agreed to stay.

Still, certain thoughts cropped up to unnerve Jim. Were local Christians clandestinely involved? He was certain that Pastor Paul Lamba faithfully resisted the movement, but he was unsure about Pastor James Ilunga. Last Sunday afternoon, just before the regular chapel hour, Jim's wife, Genny, had seen Ilunga emerge from the high grass wearing a strange-looking hat and tattered clothing. Where had he been? Soldiers had come again today, three truckloads of them. They had manhandled a few people, confiscated some livestock for food, and left. How did such incidents affect the loyalties of local people? Missionaries Charles Sprunger and Loyal Schmidt were to have brought a battery-powered transceiver that afternoon. Why had they not yet arrived? Finally, what if the missionaries should be reading the situation entirely wrong?

His thoughts were interrupted by shouts, then screams, coming from the village adjacent to the mission compound. He rushed to the window. Crackling flames from burning homes were leaping skyward. Silhouetted against them he saw the running forms of near-naked men carrying torches and primitive hand weapons.

"Genny," he called to his wife, obeying a reflex. "Bring Tim. Let's go to the car."

They went outside, Tim in pajamas. The Graber family joined them, Gladys with her hair up in curlers, she and Jeanette in night clothing. They piled into the car. Now where would they go? Rebels were taking charge of the station. Any escape was cut off. Jim recognized he had made a foolish move. He drove the short distance to the home of Pastor Lamba, where they got out. Lamba was on the verge of leaving.

"Where are you going?" Bertsche asked him.

"I'm going to see what that burning is about."

"Those are the jeunesse; the rebels. Have you forgotten?"

Selma the single-lady missionary arrived. Behind them was the sound of smashing glass. They turned to look. Rebels had broken the windows of the missionary family residences and of Graber's car and were putting them to the torch. In a fleeting mental image, Bertsche saw the Old Testament manuscript go up in flames.

Suddenly a band of about thirty screaming weapon-wielding rebels was upon them.

"Kill the pastor!" they screamed.

They brandished machetes, arrows, and spears threateningly.

"Paul Lamba. He's the one!"

"Don't you hear what they're saying?" the pastor's wife shouted at him. "Get out of here!"

Somehow Lamba escaped into the darkness.

Bible Institute buildings were now going up in flames. Kende mission station was exploding with violence.

Frenzy-crazed rebels seized the missionaries.

"Kill them! Kill them!" shouted some.

"No, wait. Wait!" shouted others.

By now missionaries were huddled inside a

wall of rebels two and three deep. Rebels inside the circle continued their harassment. They were glassy-eyed. They were perspiring profusely. They shouted and gestured incessantly. Perhaps they were high on drugs. One of them slashed the air with a honed-edge machete toward Bertsche. It landed broadside on his back. Another brandished a slender knife in the faces of his white captives, shrilling at the top of his voice, "Moscow! Moscow!" Others surrounded them closely. While haranguing, they drew arrows full-bow and held them at close range. For long dreadful moments, arrows were poised, like so many needles about to be catapulted into a cushion.

"Where is the pastor?"

"Why do you have a transmitter?"

"Who have you been talking with today?"

"Why did you call the soldiers?"

"Where is the money?"

"Why do you collaborate with the government? You're spoiling our land."

"Why are you such bad people?"

Shouts were punctuated with violence. Rebels grabbed glasses off the missionaries' faces and trampled them underfoot. They snatched women's purses and emptied men's pockets. They tore wristwatches off their arms. They pulled clothing off their bodies and hurled it back at them. They suspected that Gladys' hair curlers were a form of transmitter antenna, and they ripped them from her hair.

Suddenly the Bertsches' pup came trotting into the circle looking for Tim. A rebel slashed at it with his machete, grazing it. It yelped and scurried between legs into the darkness. Tim broke into sobs. "They're trying to hurt my puppy!"

Jim heard liquid gurgling. Rebels had found the station's store of gasoline and had rolled a drum nearby. Now they were filling a bucket from an open bung. They splashed gasoline under the fuel tank of Bertsche's vehicle and lit it. While one of them fingered a length of clothesline, others poured gasoline in a circle around the missionaries. Was the plan now to bind the white people and burn them alive, or to lynch them? In an instant they were encircled by fire.

"It was a surrealist setting," Bertsche wrote later. "We stood barefoot in the flickering light of a mission station going up in flames. We listened to the excited cries of the destroying bands, the crackling fires, the collapsing roofs, the exploding fuel drums, the hiss of a tire going suddenly flat, the blast of an igniting gas tank, the crash of shattering glass or splintering wood. And yet through these hours of greatest confusion, tension, and danger, there was a quiet reality of God's presence which was a new experience for all of us."

The encircling fire gradually burned itself out. When the jeunesse were about to resume their harassment, one with apparent authority interrupted them.

"Comrades, stay where you are."

He gestured for the missionaries to follow him. He led them to a station area which had not been disturbed and told them to sit down on the grass. When he noticed it was wet with dew, he found a mat for them to sit on. He left. After some minutes he returned and ordered them to follow him. He led them to Miss Unruh's home which was still intact. Members of his band joined him. They began to scold and harangue the missionaries.

"You white preachers shouldn't mess around in politics."

"Do you think we were happy to burn down your mission station?"

"You called soldiers to come and kill us."

"That's right. We paid you back, according to your conduct."

Their commander intervened. "We have finished our work here. We have no other affair with you. We showed you mercy by saving this house for you. Stay here until you find a way to depart."

He and his men turned and left.

The missionaries praised God that they were still alive. How good it was to take shelter in a building with its roof and doors intact! They sought to overcome the trauma of their ordeal and to recoup their energy.

Unfortunately, their rebel friend was not in command of the attack on the station that night. No one was. Every new band was its own authority with its own aims to avenge grievances.

Every new band which arrived struck Kende with a fresh shock wave of violence. About ten minutes passed, when the missionaries heard through an open window muffled voices and shuffling bare feet. Bertsche and Graber stepped outside to investigate. They were confronted by a new group of rebels standing single file, each with his bow poised on the ground before him.

Speaking in the vernacular, Bertsche greeted them and began a low-key conversation. "Are you in strength?"

"Yes. We have great strength," they replied.

"Do you want something?" Jim asked.

"We want the white women," one declared.

"Where are they?" asked others.

"How many are there?"

This new threat chilled the men. Praying fervently in their hearts, they began to talk with the raiders, casually, intimately; they had to determine the rebels' real intentions. Eventually they were able to extract a promise that the women and children would not be molested.

"Then get them out of that house so we can burn it," their leader snapped impatiently.

Women and children were brought from the house. Rebels set it on fire. Then they shoved and pushed the missionaries roughly down the path through the light of still burning buildings.

"We're taking you all to the village," the guerrillas informed them. "You men, we're taking you to our president out on the prairie tonight to be tried for your crimes."

Bertsche and Graber pondered their fate. The group reached the edge of the mission compound. Suddenly two figures dressed in white appeared. First it seemed they were angels. Then the missionaries recognized them. Male nurses in medical gowns from the dispensary had intercepted the band. They began pleading with the rebels on behalf of the missionaries. They argued. They raised their voices threateningly. After a quarter hour of heated debate the two nurses won custody of the missionaries.

"We'll pass judgment on them tonight anyhow," the leader said as he left. "We'll tell you our verdict in the morning."

The two gowned figures may have been angels after all. They took the missionaries to a small maternity hospital. They led them into an unoccupied ward. In it were three iron cots with worn split-bamboo mats covering their bare springs. A small slight widow named Julienne who had worked there for years unrolled other mats onto the concrete floor. She brought blankets from a storage closet and drinking water. The women and children eventually laid down on the cots. Jim and Harold stretched themselves out on the floor. Julienne turned down the flame of a smoky lantern on a table, pushed a chair beneath it, and left.

Bertsche couldn't sleep. He watched the orange fire glow of burning buildings dance on the room's whitewashed walls. He tried to absorb the emotional impact of the past few hours. He felt special empathy for the Grabers; previously they had been located in a different language area. Not knowing the local vernacular, they could not always follow what was going on. The foremost thought in his mind was this: through their suffering and loss they had all sensed a strong inner assurance that they were in the place of God's choosing for them. Never for a moment had that undergirding left them. Jim marveled as he recognized that only a divine restraining hand had brought them through those terrifying hours unharmed.

But it had all broken upon them so suddenly. How could they as missionaries have so misread the situation? Some of these rebels had professed to follow Christ. Most of them had benefited in some way from the mission. All of them knew what the mission stood for. What had so transformed them? It was more than drinking palm wine or smoking hemp. He had never seen people exhibit such rage, hate, vindictiveness, and cruelty. Was this wrath in some small way akin to what Jesus had felt on the cross?

Obviously the two male nurses had given some prior notice that they supported the revolution. Else how could they have blunted rebels' wrath and gained custody of the missionaries? How had Christians in the mission village fared? In this hurricane of violence and destruction, what attitude would they now take toward Christ, toward the church, and toward white missionaries? Would they renounce their faith to side with the rebels? The Bible Institute families had obeyed the missionaries' counsel. Now they were suffering. They had probably lost everything. Would they be bitter? They of all people would have reason to feel vindictive toward the missionaries.

Thinking of the missionaries, what had happened to Sprunger and Schmidt who were bringing the transceiver? As for himself and the others lying there in the ward, what was yet in store for them? How would this drama of terror finally end?

Chapter Three

Pastor Paul Lamba wandered despairingly through coarse waist-high grass on the open prairie. A high-hanging half-moon was his only light. His senses were numbed with shock. When he had first run through the receding fire glow into the darkness, he was overcome with shame. How could these deranged children, most of whom he had known all their lives, like ravaging wolves, drive him from home and scatter his people? He had rushed back to the scene of violence at his home only to be met by his wife who pummeled him with her fists and shoved him back into the darkness.

"They want to kill you!" her words still rang in his ears. "You will leave me a widow! You will orphan the children! Don't you care for us? Run! While such people are here, *don't come back!*"

At that point rebels were still abusing the missionaries. But what could he do? He had retreated to the edge of the station. He had lingered in the fringe of darkness to turn and watch. He had seen roofs of the mission buildings collapse, each in turn belching into the overhanging blackness a shower-burst of sparks to fall and die. He had listened to the terrible noises of unleashed savagery. He had stood there until convinced of the unbelievable: Kende Station, where he had invested the strength of his life, in less than an hour was destroyed.

He wandered aimlessly trying to sort out his thinking. Young Ilunga was right. He was wrong. The revolution, spreading like a wind-whipped dry season prairie fire, had reached them. Only a foolish person would resist it. Jeunesse did want to kill him. He had lived at Kende for so long. He had known those people so well. How had he failed to discern what was happening? Because he had failed to understand, he had done nothing. Now look how people suffered because they had placed their confidence in him! Missionaries who had accepted his invitation to return were now shamed and persecuted. Christian believers under his charge had been scattered like terrified sheep. All of them were refugees. And while they were suffering, he had deserted them! He had betrayed them! He, the one they all had called "Pastor"! How could they ever respect him again? How could he ever hope to be a trusted leader of people again? What purpose was still left in living? He was so filled with shame, remorse, and self-pity that the blackness of night around him was as light compared to the darkness of his soul.

He staggered ahead. He tried to pray. He lifted his arms heavenward and called out to God aloud. He wanted to share his people's sufferings. To prove it, he stripped off his shirt, his trousers, his shoes, and discarded them. He eased himself prostrate onto the ground, moaning his grief. Why could he find no peace? Then the desperate thought occurred to him. He could find peace. In death. It offered him relief from such anguish. No one would suffer more than he. He would give his life. In the dim moonlight he discerned the form of his trousers. He pulled the leather belt from the loops. He found a tree with a sturdy lower limb. Deciding to prepare his soul, he knelt and prayed.

"My God, I see that today I am dying. I am coming to You. I don't do this because I want to. How will I ever rid myself of the shame of having failed my people? And You see how these rebels are out to kill me. How can I escape them? It is best that, before they find me, I kill myself. Answer me in my heart. Am I to die, or to remain alive?"

In his bewildered mind a single thought took clear form: "How do you know you will not escape from those who seek your life? In such a case you would have killed yourself for nothing."

He took these words as an answer from God. Somehow they spoke courage and peace to his heart. God wanted him to live. He tossed his belt to the side, and sat to ponder. Yes . . . and if God gave him courage, there was still a chance that he might redeem himself. He lay down in the tall grass to rest until morning.

37

With the coming of dawn a few familiar land-marks showed him his location. He went directly to the nearest village and found the chief, a long-time friend.

"You know the rebels burned Kende station last night," Lamba said. "They threatened to kill me. I beg of you to go with me to the station this morning. I'm going to turn myself in to the rebels. Either they will kill me before the eyes of my people or they will accept me."

The chief glanced to one side and moistened his lips nervously. "This is not the time for people to be walking back and forth in the roads," he replied. "Things are not well, even in the villages. Many people have gone to live in the forest. Why don't you flee to the forest and hide with them?"

"You do not want to go with me to Kende station?"

"This is a bad time to go."

"Then stay well," Lamba replied emphatically. "I am going alone."

Chapter Four

For the missionaries held captive in the maternity ward at Kende, sleep was out of the question. They listened to the sounds of marching feet as band after band of insurgents arrived to cross the station. They would relax for brief periods of quiet, only to be jarred by the screams of renewed terrorizing. Once there were the sounds of men struggling. Then they heard the chilling thud . . . thud . . . thud of cudgel blows on a human body. Inside the ward they were sheltered by a few people who cared. Outside anarchy reigned. How could a six-inch-thick concrete wall separate two such vastly different worlds?

That separation didn't last long. Someone ripped off an outside door of the hospital building. Members of a rebel band came rushing into the ward, held lanterns high to view their white captives, made a few gloating remarks, and left. Thereafter groups came and went at will. Some were threatening, others were only curious. One of the male nurses stood in the doorway to block entry of another band.

"Stop tormenting our missionaries this way!" he protested.

Rebels threw him to the ground and beat him mercilessly. Their comrades entered unhindered.

Later again, armed guerrillas charged into the ward, their bodies streaming sweat, their eyes inflamed.

"Where is Paul Lamba?" they shouted.

"Where is Kazavubu? That traitor president . . . that ruiner of our land."

They searched under cots, inside closets, behind doors. A few with torches even climbed into the attic. Finding no one, they left.

One rebel leader entered the ward and resolutely seated himself onto the chair. Members of his group, all girls, ranged themselves along the wall around him. Reeking the odor of palm wine, he produced a blurred picture and introduced it as "the Supreme Commander of the Congo Revolution." As he propped it up on the table, he placed his ear close to it to listen intently. Suddenly he straightened himself and declared, "The Venerable One is saying. . . ." Then he launched into a voluble meandering pronouncement of rebels' grievances, all now familiar. Then he would repeat the performance, pausing to listen respectfully to the picture, and then uttering the freshly received communication.

With each succeeding wave of intruders, missionaries began to ponder the effects of this hurricane of terror. Had it swept the church completely away? Were the two male nurses and Julienne the only persons who remained to intercede for them and to minister to their needs? Answers to these questions began to take form about an hour before dawn when suddenly Louis, a carpenter, and Evariste, the mission truck driver, burst into the ward. They had cut off their pants legs and had stripped to the waist to pass for rebels. They gaped at the missionaries incredulously: the children Tim and Jeanette in pajamas, Gladys Graber in a flannel nightgown and housecoat, all the missionaries without spectacles, barefooted, dirty, and disheveled. The two black men fell onto their knees, buried their heads in their hands, and rocked back and forth sobbing. At length they regained composure to speak.

"You're still here? You are alive? Our hearts have been splitting with fear for you. We thought they had killed you. Now that we know you are alive and safe here, we're going to search for the Bible Institute families. All their homes have been burned. Everyone had fled."

The missionaries were at once saddened and heartened. Why should these two men risk their lives to help immigrant Bible Institute families whom local tribesmen considered "foreigners"? The bonds of Christian community were under terrible strain, but clearly, some of them were still intact.

Wednesday morning dawned on the missionaries and with it fearful uncertainty about their

41

fate. What had the night tribunal decided to do with them? The two male nurses left to find out. The one who had been beaten could hardly walk.

Meanwhile Christians living in Kende village, as scattered chicks regathering after the storm, returned to the charred ruins of their homes. Word spread that their missionaries were in the hospital maternity ward. They began coming by ones and twos to greet them.

"Their faces were etched with bewilderment, their eyes hollow with terror," Bertsche recalled later. "Some stood speechless. Others struggled to apologize, their voices trembling with emotion. Some simply wrapped their arms around our legs and cried like babies. Others embraced us. We stood with our arms around each other, mingling tears of gratitude that we had found each other alive."

"Here came the black woman who for many years had worked in the Graber house and who took care of Jeanette," Genny Bertsche wrote later. "She fell into Gladys Graber's arms and cried as if her heart would break. Next came a woman we had spent hours with the week before. We had consoled and encouraged her when her husband was found guilty of adultery. Tears of sympathy streamed down her face when she saw our plight. Then came Pauline, a student's wife from east across the Loange River. She was nine months pregnant. She would have to walk at least three days to get to her home area — and she came to console us! Then Bible Institute families began to arrive one by one. They too wept when they saw us; and how our hearts went out to them! We didn't sense a trace of bitterness. We had all suffered great loss together and we were each glad that the other was alive. They kept coming: ladies who attended our women's meetings, village Christians who came to church on the station on Sundays, students who had been in our classrooms. Even a few persons we had known in previous years who were now officers in the rebel ranks came to us with tears in their eyes and said, 'If we had been here last night, this would never have happened.' "

Some related their own ordeals. Pastor James Ilunga arrived, pale and stiff from being beaten. His house had been the first point of rebel attack. He had protested what guerrillas had come to do; he pleaded that they beat him if necessary, but to leave the missionaries alone. They beat him, set his house on fire, and proceeded with their raid.

Emmanuel had moved his family from their distant home area north to Kende to teach in the Bible Institute. Rebels stripped off his clothing and forced him to kneel outside his burning home. He protested their destruction of property. He refused to give them his teenage daughter. He fearlessly affirmed his innocence. When threatened for his testimony of faith, he declared his loyalty to Christ even to death. They beat him until they had vented their anger.

43

Bertsche's venerable translation consultant, David Kalau, arrived. His slender sinewy body still stood tall and straight. "There was no way of saving a thing," he said. "When they burned the house we fled into the high grass. While fleeing I prayed, 'My God, spare my typewriter.' We hunted our six children until we found them all. Then we waited hiding there. When it appeared that the attack was finished we returned to our house. We found everything burned up. Then discarded in the high grass to one side I discovered my typewriter. I don't know how it got there. God did that to show me that He still wants me to work at turning the Scriptures around into our language. When you become established again, call me. Wherever it is, I will come sit with you to continue our work."

Though misguided tribe mates had savagely abused them, Christians by loving deeds comforted one another. Their primary concern was the missionaries. A gardener brought them an avocado and a head of cabbage. A village lady who still had two dresses gave one to Gladys Graber. A local chief who appreciated the work of the mission brought a large bunch of ripening bananas. And dear Julienne — somehow she scraped things together to prepare them a hot meal of manioc mush and greens.

The missionaries were at a loss to describe their feelings about the Christian community. The rebels had terrorized these believers, had destroyed their possessions, and had scattered their children. Members of some families were still missing. Notwithstanding, these believers turned their backs on their own misfortunes, braved menacing rebel bands still crisscrossing the station, and came to affirm their loyalty to the missionaries and to the cause of Christ. Without question, the bonds of Christian community were still intact.

Suddenly in midmorning, Pastor Paul Lamba burst into the ward, his dirty body clad only in undershorts. He saw the missionaries, dropped to his knees at their feet, and sobbed into his hands, his heavy body convulsing with grief.

"Pastor! Are you still alive?" his friends exclaimed.

"Please forgive me," he sobbed. "I didn't know these things would happen."

None of them had known such things would happen. Whites and blacks consoled him.

"They're still hunting you," local believers said. "We don't want them to kill you. Let us hide you here in the hospital."

They left with him.

About ten o'clock the male nurses returned with word that local rebel groups had reached agreement: they had accomplished their objective of burning down the mission, no further moves were to be made against mission personnel, and the missionaries were to remain in custody of the male nurses until some arrangement could be made for them to leave.

During ensuing hours the Americans discussed the possibility of their being evacuated. They had not been able to broadcast at the regular time today. Surely their failure to come on the air would prompt a Missionary Aviation Fellowship pilot to come by plane and investigate.

In late afternoon the jeunesse allowed the missionaries to venture from the confines of their room for the first time. Two guerrillas escorted them. Stepping outside the hospital door, they beheld a stark strange landscape. The neat rows of homes in the village were now heaps of rubble from which protruded smoldering wall sticks. Bible Institute buildings were ruined beyond repair. Roof structures of missionary residences were collapsed. Here half exposed, there draped with crumpled partially melted aluminum sheeting, tilting peculiarly across smoke-blackened walls. The missionaries' vehicles were unfamiliar charred hulks. Of all the former mission buildings, only the hospital, one classroom building, and the chapel remained. Small groups of rebels ambled here and there; a few were starting bonfires preparing to camp for the night.

The white people learned that Bible Institute families were assembled in the chapel. They decided to go visit them. The missionaries found a few students' wives nourishing small cooking fires under a large mango tree near the chapel entrance. Others were inside lying on church benches or seated on the concrete floor. Suddenly they recognized the arrival of visitors.

"What a good thing! Our missionaries have come to greet us!" Men and women stood and reached across the clutter of blanket-wrapped bundles and battered suitcases to shake their hands warmly. "Do you have any news?"

The white visitors found places to sit down.

"Just that rebel leaders say they have no further affair with people of the mission," Jim said. "We are to sit quietly until a way can be arranged for us to leave."

Students nodded understandingly. Their eyes hung upon him. Then Bertsche realized that they were waiting for an answer to the question which logically followed.

"And when a way is arranged for us to leave," he added, "I assure you that we will only go out all of us together. We will not abandon you." The students had followed the missionary counsel and were now bearing its harsh consequences, he mused. He would do all in his power to see that it did not happen again.

"And while we wait, look how we're all suffering, like one person, together," a student observed philosophically.

"There are still some people at this place with hearts of courage for the cause of God," one said affirmingly. "Have you heard how Christians entered the high grass of the valley hunting us? We and our children were like chicken feathers scattered by the wind. They searched until they found every one of us. Then they arranged with leaders of the rebels for us to stay here."

"On top of that," another said, "Pastor James Ilunga gathered people together for prayer meeting this afternoon. Did you hear him beating the calling drum? He feared no one. We met right over there." The man motioned toward a small grass-roofed shelter spared by the holocaust.

"Preacher," another announced to Bertsche, "we have been talking among ourselves about this study business. We want you to know that if the rebels have destroyed our school buildings, they have not destroyed our wanting to learn from the Book of God."

"That's right!" others jerked their heads affirmatively.

"After we leave this place our desire is to gather ourselves together again somewhere else, no matter where, to continue our studies," said another.

"We don't need nice buildings and benches," affirmed a third. "Just give us a roof to shelter our heads from the rain, notebooks and pencils, and you can keep right on teaching us."

"There is a different matter about which we feel ashamed," another announced. "We are not happy to see our white people walking around with bare feet. I have a pair of shoes I think would fit one of you." He began struggling with the stubborn latch of a suitcase.

"No. No," the missionaries protested simultaneously. "Don't do that. It is no matter. You have

48

only a few things left. Keep them."

"No, he has spoken well," others affirmed. "You white people have soft feet. Ours are tough. When the time comes for us to leave, how will you walk rapidly?"

"Take these. Put them on your feet."

The man had pulled two shoes from the suitcase and was extending them toward Bertsche. They were warped, without laces, and the color of sometime gray. Their heels were run-down, their toes were scuffed, their soles had holes. Jim took them.

Meanwhile, other men and their wives rummaged through their meager belongings. They extracted an amazing assortment of shoes. They kept exchanging pairs between white bare feet until every missionary had a pair. Bertsche's proved about a size too small. He jammed his feet into them nonetheless. He would never spurn such a gift.

"Here, Mama," one of the women said to Genny Bertsche. She had pulled from her bundle a sweater worn through at the elbows, most of its buttons missing. "Take this. It is cool at night."

Genny took it gratefully.

Then they set themselves to repacking their belongings.

The missionaries marveled how tribulation had fostered loving concern for one another. They thanked their friends, prayed with them, and then, freshly encouraged, returned to the maternity ward for the night.

It had been a long day for Paul Lamba hiding in the small hospital room. Shortly after dark he heard the angry voices of approaching rebels. They were shouting his name. Apparently word had leaked that he was hiding there. The rebels' shouting sounded as if they had surrounded the building. Suddenly the room door opened. It was one of his church elders.

"Pastor, come."

The man led Lamba to a rear door. "You can escape this way. When I open the door, flee."

The elder opened the door. Paul raced into the darkness, stumbled, and fell. Suddenly thunder boomed and a rainstorm broke. Lamba saw it as God's means of confusing his pursuers. He picked himself up and ran through drenching rain into the high grass toward the valley.

This was the first of new rebel groups which came to visit the hospital that night. Apparently news of last night's events had spread, bringing insurgents from greater distances. Again, sleep was impossible for the missionaries. Periodically rebels came into the ward armed with hand weapons, their short pants and bare bodies dripping rain. They would harangue the Americans, bang their way through the building in search of President Kazavubu, or some other purported enemy, and then pass on.

About midnight the missionaries again heard the arrival of visitors. Wearily they glanced toward the door and saw a rebel with their missing

50

colleagues, Charles Sprunger and Loyal Schmidt. The men were rain-drenched and exhausted but alive. The Kende missionaries jerked themselves upright to gaze in wonder and gratitude.

"I am vice-president of the jeunesse in this area," the rebel announced. "I have brought your relatives." Then followed a long familiar discourse explaining why it had been necessary for insurgents to destroy the Kende mission station.

As soon as he left, the missionaries rejoiced at their reunion. Then Sprunger and Schmidt related their 70-hour ordeal in the hands of insurrectionists. On their trip with the transceiver they were intercepted by a company of some forty rebels. Their hands were bound behind them. Three stripped teenagers, holding knife-points to the missionaries' backs, forced them to fast-trot for miles toward a guerrilla camp headquarters. Once an old wrinkled chief refused to give these teenagers aid. When they threatened to burn down his village he fell to his knees, cowering at their feet, pleading pardon. He was shown mercy, and then ordered food prepared for them.

They arrived at guerrilla headquarters late at night. A milling mob of about 800 rebels gloated over the captured white men, some calling for their death. Sprunger ran the gauntlet of five examiners. Each in turn interrogated him ruthlessly while five arrows drawn full-bow were held a foot from his head and a knife was poised at his neck. Then Schmidt was interrogated in the same manner. When examiners found no conflict in the missionaries' testimonies, they declared them innocent. Then, escorted by the vice-president, the two men completed the 35-mile foot trek to Kende.

Five examiners interrogated Sprunger ruthlessly with arrows drawn full-bow held a foot from his head.

About eleven o'clock on Thursday morning the missionaries heard the roar of an approaching motor. They rushed outside to see. It was a Missionary Aviation Fellowship plane. It circled slowly, banked and turned, and then circled a second time, dropping a note. Tim Bertsche, still in his pajamas, raced to get it. He returned with it. The missionaries clustered to read it.

"Signal if you can make a short strip for me to land."

The captives were in no position to make that kind of decision. They stood motionless.

The plane kept circling. Finally it turned and made a low pass dropping another note:

"If you think a helicopter could land, sit down."

They sat down onto the ground.

The plane circled, tipped a wing to acknowledge having received the message, and left.

Immediately four rebels came rushing from the high grass, sweating, swinging their machetes, irrational with anger.

"Who called that airplane?"

"What did you tell them?"

"Who among you has a transmitter in his pocket?"

"We've treated you well. Now you are calling the soldiers again?"

They tore at missionaries' clothing and ransacked their pockets. The white people patiently explained why the plane had come, that the jeunesse leaders had agreed to their evacuation, and that they were merely making arrangements for it. Finally a group leader came. He was a relative of a prominent Christian. He produced a penciled scrap of paper authorizing himself to take command of activities on Kende station. He asserted his authority and brought the assailants to reason.

"All right," they finally agreed. "But you know we have made a covenant. When that plane comes, if there is a government soldier on it, we're cutting off your heads. Not a one of you will remain alive."

The leader commanded his company of sixty guerrillas to police the compound and maintain order. Later he confided to Bertsche that he was sick about what had happened to the station. He and his superiors had determined that the whites would suffer no more ill treatment and would be evacuated as soon as possible. He ordered a local chief to produce machetes and hoes to use to clear a landing strip. The missionaries began to breathe more easily. This man seemed to exercise authority. They took the tools and set to work to clean a 350-yard stretch of road. That afternoon Bible Institute students were allowed to help them. The rebels watched from the sidelines. Occasionally one would catch the missionaries' attention and menacingly draw a forefinger across his throat. They finished cleaning the strip about four o'clock. Then, using manioc flour and rolls of white muslin bandages, they blocked out a message in two-foot-high letters:

OK TO LAND 350 YARDS BRING NO SOLDIERS SAFETY ASSURED

"I wonder which women's auxiliary in America sent us these bandages?" Genny speculated, as they carefully laid the white strips in place.

"How would the dear lady who made these rolls feel if she knew what we were using them for now?" Gladys remarked.

They returned to the maternity ward dead tired. They had gone for sixty hours with little sleep. Someone brought them a few cans of food salvaged from the debris of one of their homes. Julienne cooked them a meal of mush and chicken. Armed sentries were posted outside hospital doors. The missionaries prepared for their first night of rest.

Before retiring, Bertsche noticed that Tim was morose.

"What's the matter, son?"

"I haven't seen my dog for two days." He

stared into space. "I wonder if he's hungry."

Friday morning came. The missionaries were up at daybreak. They went and checked the lettering. Then they sat down to wait. They agreed that if an evacuation craft came, women and children, black and white should go first. The hours drug by. Band after band of sweating nervous rebels arrived. They took up positions by groups in the high grass along the makeshift airstrip. Word had spread that the white people had called a plane; and rebels were coming in force to make good their threat, should the plane bring soldiers. Tension mounted. The friendly guerrilla leader seemed increasingly apprehensive. It appeared he feared losing command of the situation. The sun was hot. The grass teemed with ill-concealed rebels.

Noon had just passed when they heard the drone of approaching aircraft. Tension climbed. Shortly a plane arrived and began a low circling pattern. Then two United Nations helicopters came flying just above the trees.

Instantly the atmosphere was taut as a drumhead.

The rebels crouched silently in the grass watching.

The copters hovered over the nearby soccer field, their motors roaring. Slowing they set down. Their whirling rotors churned up huge clouds of dust. Bertsche rushed through the dust cloud to the nearest copter and climbed a fuselage ladder to talk with the pilot.

"Take out our families and these Bible Institute women and children first," he shouted above the engine noise. "We men will go out on your next trip."

The white pilot gestured helplessly and shook his head, answering in very broken English. Bertsche was trying desperately to communicate his message when suddenly the pilot was speaking into a mike. Apparently the crew of the hovering plane was relaying to him news of some rebel activity which forced him to abandon all other considerations. He yelled an order to his crewmen. They began dragging missionaries bodily into the craft. Bertsche dropped off the ladder and was pulled inside.

Jim rapidly took count and discovered that Sprunger was missing. Looking out, he discerned through the dust the forms of two rebels struggling with a missionary. A crewman grabbed a submachine gun from a wall bracket and leaped onto the ground. The rebels released the man. The craft was already airborne. Sprunger rushed to the open door. He and the crewman were dragged inside.

The copter transported the Americans to a mission post in a safe area east across the Loange River and immediately returned to evacuate the Bible Institute families. A missionary host showed the Bertsche family to a guest room, where they bathed. Then Genny and Tim went to bed. But Jim couldn't relax until he learned what had happened on the second evacuation flight. Word came toward evening. When the copters returned they found the landing strip obstructed with posts set upright in the ground. There was no way of landing. People there gestured that the Bible Institute families had left on foot.

Bertsche felt a sense of personal despair. Before the attack the families had agreed to abide by missionary counsel to remain at Kende rather than to evacuate to their home areas. Now, in spite of his best intentions, it appeared that the missionaries had left them in the lurch a second time. They would have to try and escape on foot now. It would be a long and hazardous trek. He thought of what was in store for the women and small children. He thought of Pauline, nine months pregnant. Then he thought of the shoes. These poor people. Not only were they deprived of quick evacuation by helicopter but they were even deprived of their shoes — seven pairs of them.

These Bible Institute families were tribal aliens; he hoped they would get out. But what was the future of the thousands of Christians native to the strife-torn region? At first many of them had identified with the spirit of the revolution, but already they felt betrayed. After the rebels destroyed Kende the believers had told Jim repeatedly, "This was not supposed to happen. We weren't told it would be like this." They had no way of escaping it. They were caught in it. How would they react toward it? Jim pondered the alternatives: a believer could resist the movement at the risk of bodily harm or death; or he could work to reform the movement from within and where necessary violate his Christian conscience; or he could compromise by giving tacit loyalty to whatever group seemed to hold power. Any course a believer chose was full of danger.

Chapter Five

Stephen Kimeya, born of Christian parents, had grown up in the large village adjacent to the mission station of Mudidi. Since childhood he had known the missionaries well. While in primary school he had worked as a "house boy" in a missionary home. Following secondary and normal training, Stephen taught school for a number of years. His unswerving integrity had earned him high esteem. Now he was about twenty-five years of age and married, with two small daughters. Medium in height, stocky in build, with eyes deep-set in a somewhat pudgy face, Stephen's quiet demeanor concealed an inner core of resolve as hard as steel. He was administrator of a network of primary schools, in charge of daily radio broadcasts of mission business and a key layman in the station church council.

Kimeya sat in the bright morning sunlight in front of his simple concrete block home waiting for his wife, Sona, to bring him a cup of tea. His two girls, in pretty print dresses, were playing peekaboo around a front doorjamb. He envied the innocence of childhood. It allowed children to play lightheartedly at times when their parents must carry grave responsibility. He had been with Jim Bertsche at the distant church administrative meeting when the radio message came advising them of deteriorating conditions and urging them to return home. He had felt the growing crush of responsibility ever since. Why must such an affair disrupt their lives? Like a green mango, it made his stomach ache.

Pierre Mulele, commanding general of the revolution, was of the Bambunda tribe. Kende and Mudidi were located in the area of a larger tribe living adjacent to the Bambunda. A man named Mazemba was chief of the large village at Mudidi and of satellite hamlets immediately surrounding it. Their total population exceeded five thousand. Mazemba and most of his people were strongly sympathetic with the aims of the rebellion and gave it at least their passive support. At the outset Kimeya himself had been open-minded toward it. Now, as he watched the movement take form, he had misgivings.

This was Saturday. How could so many things happen in so short a time? When Kimeya arrived home a week ago he learned that Mulelists had set up a "zone command headquarters" in a village six miles from Mudidi. A foreign tribesman was put in charge of it. Thereafter insurrectionists became increasingly bold in their destructive forays. On Wednesday night one band razed a government post twelve miles away and massacred some of its personnel; another band destroyed a Catholic mission.

On Thursday armed insurgents arrived at Mudidi. In broad daylight they began massing along the station airstrip. The missionaries met with local church leaders to decide on a course of action. Kimeya, voicing the consensus of the leaders, said, "We would like for you white people to stay, but you had better leave. Things are very bad. If you commit us into the hands of the Lord, we will pass through them and survive." Then they sang together, "We'll Work Till Jesus Comes." Everybody was crying. The missionaries left keys to their homes and vehicles with Kimeya. A distress call was sent by radio.

Two small planes came answering the call. One of the pilots brought news that he had flown over Kende station and found it burned; its missionaries were standing outside the hospital building. Chief Mazemba loaded his shotgun. He and his armed sons held the rebels at bay while the two planes lifted out the missionaries. With the departure of the missionaries, rebels withdrew. But Kimeya's troubles had only begun.

Shortly thereafter Chief Mazemba came demanding that Kimeya give him the keys to the missionary property. Kimeya adamantly refused, accusing the chief of collaborating with those who would destroy the mission. Mazemba was furious. He returned repeatedly, mounting an attack of personal threats against Kimeya. After a series of volatile exchanges Kimeya capitulated and gave him the keys. Now sentries, all close male relatives of Mazemba, guarded missionary residences. Kimeya suspected the chief's motives. The incident left the two of them bitterly estranged.

His thoughts were interrupted when his wife, Sona, arrived. She was a heavy woman slightly taller than he. She handed him a cup of sweet tea and returned to the cooking hut behind their home. He was waiting for the tea to cool when he noticed eight young men, empty-handed and dressed only in short pants, approaching in the road which passed in front of his home. Some of the men were familiar. His eyes followed them as they arrived at the path leading to his house, turned into it, and approached him.

"Did you sleep well?" they greeted him.

"Yes. Are you with strength?"

"We are with strength."

"Do you have a word to speak?"

"Yes," said one of them. He stepped forward to assume the role of spokesman. "We have come from the zone command headquarters. Our president says that, seeing the white people have left, he no longer plans to attack Mudidi station. He sends us with peace. He says that the bow and arrow must respect each other and by working together they kill the prey. So if the people of Mudidi work together with us, the revolution will move forward without hindrance."

His comrades nodded assentingly.

"All of us are like beans cooking in a pot," he

continued. "The plight of one is the plight of all. Do I need to describe for you our suffering? For forty years we lived under the rule of the white man. When independence came we rejoiced surpassingly. The white man's rule ended. Now we would share it among us. The wealth of our country would no longer fill the pockets of foreigners. It would serve us all. We would have schools. We would have places to work."

His friends grunted affirmingly.

"Three years have passed now since we received independence," he continued. "What single good thing has come from it? Those black leaders of ours, what one good thing have they done for us? Have they built a school? Have they built a hospital? Our teachers, why aren't they paid? Why are medicines in our dispensaries all finished? Why are the roads ruined having sandpits and gullies? Why are shelves in stores empty of things we need? Why are things like this? Because President Kazavubu and his helpers have taken the wealth of our land and stuffed it into their pockets."

"Speak!" some urged.

"Tell it plainly!" the others prodded.

"Those sitting in chairs of chieftainship are greedy. They are like chickens scratching with both feet. They don't pity us the tiniest bit. They dress in suits and neckties while poverty dresses us with loincloths. They ride in big black cars which sparkle in the sun while we walk. They fill their bellies every day with whatever food they desire while we fail to have salt for our mush. Their children go to universities across the great water while youth like us — thousands which surpass being counted — fail to find places in high school. This is capitalism! See how the rich torment the poor! They are pounding us like berries in a mortar! They want to drink every drop of our juice and then discard the rinds!"

"Truth!"

"That's the way it is!" His colleagues were gesturing spiritedly.

"How do we change such affairs?" he continued. "Take such traitors to court? If I go to court and accuse a superior of injustice, he bribes the judge; the judge finds me guilty and throws me into prison. My adversary keeps on paying the judge so that I never get out. How many of our tribesmates thus languish in prison? Count them! Will they remain in their cold cells forever? When people of a village complain the government calls it 'a revolt.' Soldiers come. They ask who is stirring us up. They beat us. They steal our livestock. They leave us poorer than ever. There is no way that we by ourselves can change things. For this reason we rejoice surpassingly for the return of Pierre Mulele. Because of him we have hope! He has come with wisdom to help us. He will liberate us! He will open the path for us to go forward again!"

"Mulele o-yay-eee! Mulele o-yay-eee!" his comrades chanted, driving their clenched fists skyward.

64

"What is the wisdom of Mulele for changing things? We decide to take over a piece of the country. We sever the roads and disable ferries so government soldiers cannot come to interfere with what we need to do. Then we burn down government posts. People who rule in such places have become fat with the money of Kazavubu. Some of them flee. Others join us. Their chairs of authority are left empty. Then leaders of the revolution take their places and begin to rule. Our comrades will bring the wealth of everybody into one treasure. Afterwards they will divide it out to all people equally. By this means everyone will share the good things of independence. Then our suffering will end."

Kimeya got up, put his empty cup onto the veranda behind him, and sat down again. He would patiently hear them out.

"Soon the rule of Kazavubu will end. Don't you see how rapidly the revolution has spread? All the people in the villages want it. Those few greedy rulers and their slaves whom they call 'soldiers' — how will they stop it? Those soldiers are fighting for pay. We are fighting for the land of our tribal ancestors. Our ancestors' spirits who live in the earth beneath our feet are fighting with us. They groan that our earth is so ruined. Because they are helping us, we don't need things foreigners have made. That is why soldiers cannot stop us. They wear thick clothing and heavy shoes and carry weapons from foreigners. With our bare feet on the ground, our ancestral spirits give us their strength. They make our arrows more powerful than white men's guns. With the wisdom of Mulele and the help of our ancestors we do things which surpass the mind to comprehend. After we have destroyed those who have betrayed us — after we have wiped the land clean of their pollution — then the wrath of our ancestral spirits will be appeased; then the friends of Mulele, his teachers, will come help us build our land."

He paused and looked intently at Kimeya.

"You are a man of much wisdom. You have influence. We need your help. If you join us, your friends will follow behind you. What is your thinking?"

Kimeya weighed his reply carefully. The alternatives were stark.

"All of us see the torment of our land," he began. "We long for this suffering to end. But your words say that changing these things is as easy as breaking a twig. Are you certain that this path will not multiply the suffering of us all?"

"How could it?" the rebel leader countered. "All of us are already in the path of death. What is the difference whether a witch doctor kills us with fleabites, or with tatters of poverty? Tell me, is there anything left for us to lose? True, the revolution causes some people to suffer. Our elders say that one cannot clean a long-neglected pot without causing it pain. You sit in your home. You play with your children. You sleep with your wife. Look at us. We sleep in the forest or in the high grass. We are denying ourselves. We are suffering. But we are not suffering for nothing. Those who refuse to follow the wisdom of Mulele and refuse to do what pleases our ancestral spirits, they will suffer surpassingly."

There was an uncomfortable silence.

"I cannot make such a decision alone," Stephen finally said. "I must talk with my wife and my clansmen."

The spokesman frowned. He did not like procrastination.

"I want to inform you that I am begging you to join us not only to strengthen the movement, but for your own sake."

The words jogged Kimeya's attention.

"Explain what you mean."

"There are many who believe that your own hands are not clean. They say that you helped the missionaries escape. You send messages on the transceiver to frustrate the revolution. Because you are a school administrator, you handle money from Kazavubu. You collaborate with his people. Teachers accuse you of not paying the salaries due them. People say you have your nice house and other possessions because of hoarding wealth you've received from Kazavubu. We would not want something bad to happen to you or to your family. You should join us so that we can take upon ourselves the responsibility of protecting you from those who would do you ill."

The words were a poorly veiled threat. Some

of these accusations were clearly false. Kimeya had been performing his job responsibly; he had nothing to be ashamed of. He suspected that the rebels had nurtured grievances of a few dissident teachers and now they were exploiting the support of these dissidents to coerce him. He could join the movement, and if he did, many people at Mudidi likely would follow him. At the same time, certain elements of the movement disturbed him deeply. He could not agree with its violence. He could not agree with its animosity toward white people and particularly toward the missionaries. Why did it require the expulsion of the missionaries unless it recognized that their teachings opposed methods it felt to be necessary? How does one build by killing and destroying? How would he live with his conscience when the ideology which motivated such conduct so violated Christian truth? Finally, Kimeya had a stubborn streak. He resented being coerced into doing anything. He would refuse to join now, if for no other reason than that they had threatened him with blackmail.

"This is the first time anyone has talked with me about these matters," he replied calmly. "Does a hunter berate his dog for not immediately pursuing a trail? I cannot decide at this moment what course to follow. I need some days to think. I have no other word now."

"As you wish," the spokesman said. "But don't waste time. The revolution is progressing rapidly. Something bad could happen if its leaders decided that you were standing in its way. We will give you a few days. Then we will return for your answer."

The group turned and left the way it had come.

Stephen Kimeya knew these men were not playing with words. They were dead serious. In spite of their threats, he did not see how he could openly support the movement. Perhaps he should compromise with it. But compromise would mean plaguing indecision, unpredictable entanglements, and a protesting conscience. This seemed to leave him with a single option: to resist it.

At this point it was a lonely stand to take. He was already at odds with Mazemba their chief. Now he would also be at odds with the insurrectionists. They and Mazemba would count him their common enemy. What price would such a stand exact from him? Would church leaders align with him, or follow Mazemba? Such a stand could cost him his life. If such were the case, he could take consolation in one thought; others before him had died for their faith in Christ; and martyrdom would convince those watching that some truths are important enough to die for.

If his fate was uncertain, one thing was clear: a moment of reckoning with leaders of the revolution was inevitable. Meanwhile, until that time, he would drink deeply of the blessings which still were his — the love of his wife — the joy of his children — and the support of Christian believers who he believed would stand with him through crisis.

Chapter Six

Pastor James Ilunga slowly walked at the head of the long line of Bible Institute refugees. He wore only short pants and carried in his hand a knob-topped walking stick which, when held by its small end, could serve as a club. Close behind him trudged David Kalau, a church elder and Bertsche's veteran translation assistant. With one hand Kalau supported a small child on his hip and with the other he led a larger child on foot. Behind him followed a twelve-year-old son; the lad carried on his head a typewriter.

Then followed a bedraggled band of fifty-four persons: ten men, eleven women (two of them pregnant including Pauline who was now full term), twenty children old enough to walk, and thirteen children so small they needed to be carried. Older persons, on their shoulders, on their heads, on their hips, and on a few overworn bicycles, carried their possessions: here a portable sewing machine, there a lantern, rolled sleeping mats, a few chickens tied by the feet, battered suitcases, and variously shaped blanket bundles containing kitchen utensils, books, and clothing.

They were on a long and perilous trek which Ilunga hoped would lead his friends to safety. He could think of good reasons why he should have stayed at home. His body was still sore from the beating that night when the rebels burned Kende station. The jeunesse had destroyed his home and possessions. They still harassed his people. In one sense it was sheer foolishness for a man to renounce his duties to his clan, to his wife, and to his six small children at a moment as crucial as this, and endanger his life to save a band of immigrants.

Notwithstanding, Ilunga felt a keen sense of responsibility for these people. There is a traditional law of hospitality among his people which says that a village chief must give haven to a stranger coming for help and to see him on his way, lest some peril befall the man and his relatives come and ask the chief why. James Ilunga had been the leading professor of local origin at the Bible Institute. In a sense he was their chief and was accountable for their safety. It was his duty to help them toward their destination.

But a more impelling reason for helping them was that they were his brothers and sisters in Christ. If these alien refugees traveled alone, they would almost certainly fall prey to some undisciplined rebel band and be massacred. In such a case he would carry their blood on his hands all the rest of his life and to a day of reckoning before his Lord. His family did have needs. His clansmen would have contemptuous questions. He would confront these issues later. For now, helping this group of people must come first.

He would do his utmost to get them through the immediate more populated region where hazard was greatest to where they could safely continue on their own, eastward to the Loange River which bordered onto their homeland. He was not at all certain that he would succeed. These were evil days. Such days demanded that Christians show their courage. He had learned that social disorder often came with the transfer of political power. But these days of trouble should not last too long. This revolution had gained such momentum that those rising to oppose it were almost certainly doomed to defeat. In his thinking, the incumbent national government was too bankrupt to survive, it would soon collapse and the revolutionary government would take control.

He recognized that the change would not be easy for Christians. The new government would do things contrary to their beliefs. But they would simply have to adapt themselves to the new order of things. Had it not been the same with first-century Christians? They had been compelled to live under the hostile rule of Rome. They lived with the system, continued to silently do their work, and in the end, changed it. If this happened then, could it not happen now?

But at this point, there was no authority in the land. To a large degree, each wandering group of insurrectionists was a law unto itself. Pastor Ilunga and the Bible Institute families had left Kende yesterday afternoon, after they had watched guerrillas plant posts in the football field to prevent a second landing of helicopters. Upon leaving he had given the refugees strict instructions. In case of confrontation, those who could not speak the local vernacular perfectly were to remain silent. There was to be no sign which would betray their identity as strangers. He, a native of the region, would try to mediate for the group. When the group needed food and shelter, he would stop at villages where he knew there were Christians; he was certain they would do their utmost to help. Such had proven to be the case last night. While in the road, he would maintain the lead position, because the fate of the leader probably would be the fate of them all.

It was Saturday now. They were on open prairie. The sun was high and hot. The narrow sandy road, hemmed in on either side by a wall of grass, meandered ahead of them like an endless corridor. As he rounded a bend the pastor caught sight of three armed rebels in the road ahead of them. They had seen him. It was too late to attempt flight. The rebels froze their positions and held half-drawn bows in a ready position.

"Are you a partisan?" one of them called.

"I am a partisan," Ilunga replied.

"What is the name of your group?"

"The group of Kende."

"What is the name of your regional president?"

The pastor called back the name without faltering.

"Stay where you are."

From the grass alongside the road emerged a band of about forty armed guerrillas. Cautiously they approached, discovered the full group of refugees, and quickly encircled them.

"These are not partisans," the leader confronted the pastor. "They are fugitives. You are lying to me. You are leading these people to defect to the soldiers of Kazavubu."

"That is not true," Ilunga countered. "I am a partisan. Members of the Kende group were consulting with me days before Kende was burned. Ask me their names. Ask me the names of the regional leaders of the revolution. I will tell you. These men were studying at Kende. I am taking them and their families home."

People had put down their backbreaking loads. The pregnant women sat down in the road. Mothers untied waist cloths which bound infants to their backs or pacified crying babies at their breasts. The men stood listening, weighing their fate. Older children, their eyes big and white with fear, clung to their fathers' legs.

"Are they partisans?" the group leader nodded toward the men.

"As I already said, they are students. We ourselves called them to come to Kende to study. Why should they join the movement at Kende?

Now I am taking them to their homes. When they get there, the jeunesse leaders in their home areas will recruit the men into their groups."

"How do I know that you are not deceiving me?" the rebel leader snarled.

"I already asked you to interrogate me. If I cannot answer your questions about the movement, then you will know that I am deceiving you."

"We will interrogate those men, those fugitives. We will interrogate them one by one. Then we will establish the truth of the matter."

"You will not interrogate those men. I am their leader. You have no right to override my authority. If the leader of another group wanted to override yours, what would you say? When you refuse to interrogate me, you reveal that you have already purposed to do us ill."

"We would do no one ill without first trying to determine whether or not he is guilty."

"That is what I am asking you to do," Ilunga countered. "Try me. If you find me guilty, then you can do with me and all these people as you wish. But you need to know that these people have already been tried. The group president at Kende arrested them, tried them, and found them innocent. The court decided that they could be released to go to their homes. I accepted to lead them. If you now stand in the way of my carrying out the decision of the court, then you are obstructing a directive of the revolution. When the news of your conduct reaches Kende, you alone must bear the consequences."

The leader paused and then mellowed.

"It is no affair, comrade," he said, motioning for his men to stand aside. "Be on your way."

Slowly the refugees reorganized themselves and continued their journey. Out of sight of the guerrilla band they stopped to pray. They thanked God for His deliverance and implored His protection for the long road ahead. They continued their slow trek until after sundown when they arrived at a grassy sward sheltered by a large tree on the edge of a village.

"Sit down here to wait for me," Pastor Ilunga told them. "I'll go see if these people will keep us tonight."

By inquiring he found his way to the chief's house. The chief greeted him and showed him a chair. He sat down.

"I am a pastor from Kende," he began. "I am in the path with a group of students. I am leading them in the direction of the Loange River so they can return home. If I remember well, some of my friends sit here in your village."

James recited the names of three Christian men whom he had met during previous years in school. The chief was honored that his esteemed visitor remembered that they lived in his village.

"The people I am with are owners of good hearts," the pastor continued. "They are students of the Book of God. We have been walking all day. Among us are little children. We need your help."

"How many are there?"

"About twenty grown-ups and their children."

The chief pondered the problem. "I had in mind to receive these guests at my house. But this is a large group. It is necessary that I consult the elders of my village to arrange a means of carrying this responsibility."

Ilunga sighed with relief. This chief would help them.

The chief sent children to call the elders and Ilunga's three Christian friends. When the believers arrived they warmly greeted the pastor and stood around his chair. Four elders came and squatted in a semicircle in front of the chief, folding their arms across their knees. The chief opened the conversation and explained the problem. The elders probed the visitor with questions, heard his replies, and weighed how to respond.

"It is a hard affair to entertain strangers these days," one elder said dubiously.

"That is true," the others affirmed nodding their heads.

"Maybe these strangers are being hunted by the military," a second elder suggested. "How can we know? After we care for them and they leave, soldiers may come and beat us. Or maybe guerrillas are hunting them; after they go on their journey, the jeunesse will come and burn down our houses. It is best that we not get mixed up in this matter, then no one will come afterwards and torment us."

There was a pause. Tension was mounting.

"Are you saying that we will drive away strangers who have come in need?" one believer replied incredulously. "We are your juniors. Why should it be necessary for us to teach you the proverbs of our ancestors? They said, 'Listen to the pleas of women and children or the day will come when no one will listen to yours. Giving is not losing, it is storing; someday it will return to you.'"

"Our chief did not ask you if we would help these strangers," said another. "He asked your wisdom on how we would share the responsibility."

The two groups divided sharply on the issue. Finally the three Christians moved in to stand close to the pastor. One spoke for them all.

"We want to establish before you that as people of Christ we are one flesh and bone with Pastor Ilunga. We and his people are all of the same family — the family of faith. You can decide what you like. As for us, we are obeying our tribal ancestors who said, 'Feed the orphan; he is an offspring of the Almighty.' We are obeying the words of our Lord Jesus Christ when He said, 'Love one another.' Afterwards, if people of this village suffer because we have been kind to strangers, we Christians will bear the burden of it in our own bodies. If we die, let us die."

People sat silent absorbing the impact of these words. Finally the chief spoke.

"I am giving the order for each of you elders to

have women in your part of the village prepare three loaves of mush and a pot of meat. I will greet the guests at my house and keep them here while you prepare things. Later, I will divide the people into four groups and send one group to each of you. I will keep the pastor and one family at my house. You will see that everyone in your group has food and a place to sleep. Let us go to begin our work."

The refugees ate and slept well that night. The following day was Sunday. They had a brief worship service with the small group of village believers, drank hot tea which had been prepared for them, and resumed their journey. They picked up fragments of news from all who passed. Rumors were rife: Government soldiers were approaching and people were fleeing to the forests. The rebels ahead were killing all strangers; the refugees' only hope was to establish contact with a more sympathetic guerrilla band which might offer them protection. Pastor James successfully handled another hostile confrontation with a roving band of rebels. In spite of mounting fears of what may lie before them, they plodded steadily on.

They were on a treeless stretch of prairie and the sun was almost straight up when they reached a fork in the path. They unloaded their burdens to rest.

"We need to choose which way we will take," Ilunga said. "Along the left-hand path there are numerous villages. There are trees for shade and people from whom we can beg food. The right-hand path follows across the prairie. There are no people living along it. There are no trees. There is no water that way. It is some shorter. The journeyer who walks this path without resting can reach the village at the Loange River before the sun goes down."

People were tired. They began to argue heatedly. Those who wanted to take the left-hand path seemed to prevail; in that direction there was some hope of aid. Finally David Kalau, the oldest member of the party, raised his hand to command silence.

"It is true that in the left-hand path are villages and people and shelter and food. But that is also where guerrilla bands are doing their work. Our fathers said, 'Do you go ask an angry lion where he got his pretty mane?' Up to this point God has heard our prayers. He has taken care of us. Why should we now hunt trouble? The path which looks easy is not always the path of wisdom. We must do all we can to take care of ourselves, then we can leave the rest with God. The right-hand path leads us across prairie. It will be hot. We will get thirsty. If we follow the other path, the rebels may kill us. The heat and thirst of this half a day need kill none of us. If we strengthen our hearts and God hears our pleas, we will reach the river tonight."

"In my mind Elder Kalau has spoken well," Ilunga rejoined. "Inasmuch as we are far from Kende now, I do not know the villages of that path well. It would be difficult for us to find friends there who would help us. Long ago God helped His children pass through the wilderness. Let us trust Him. He will help us too."

With a few dissenting murmurs people began to stir, took fresh courage, loaded their burdens, and entered the wilderness path.

They trekked slowly, perseveringly, through the hot hours of the afternoon. They wondered where strength came from to keep them going. They saw few people. They met no danger. When Pastor Ilunga James saw that all was now going well, he concluded that he had fulfilled his obligation; the refugees could safely continue on their own. He had final prayer with them. They thanked him profusely, said goodbye to him, and watched him begin the journey alone back to Kende. Elder David Kalau replaced Pastor Ilunga at the head of the line as it moved slowly, persistently eastward.

The sun rested like a huge orange ball on the horizon that Sunday evening when the first members of the straggling line crested a hill, discovered the outskirts of a village to their left, and saw the meandering silt-red waters of the Loange River in the valley before them. David Kalau went to establish contact with people in the village. Others put down the bundles and children they had been carrying and returned to help those following behind. Elder David and some of the refugee families were tribally akin to the people here, they could speak the language perfectly. But his special concern was for those families whose tribes were totally alien to this area.

Gratefully he discovered that the people were friendly. If they were not Christian, they were humane. Residents in huts nearest the road received the travelers, arranged sitting places for them on mats or on chairs, and brought them water and available edibles. All seemed to be going well. Then a group of young men approached and stood watching them. Suddenly one of the group announced, "We don't know who you are; but if there are foreign tribesmen among you, they will never cross that river."

Fear stabbed the refugees' hearts like a dagger; they dared not betray its pain. They remained stolid, indifferent. David Kalau groped for a means of coping with this new threat.

"Didn't you hear what we said?" the man asked testily.

"My friend, we arrived only now," Elder Kalau replied calmly. "Are you failing to remember words of our forefathers? They said, 'Don't ask a stranger what is in his stomach until you have given him something to eat.' " Then, looking directly at the village man whose attitude had been most cordial, he continued. "Inasmuch as you have already welcomed us so kindly, it is time that you take me to greet your chief." He hoped other villagers who had shown hospitality would feel responsible to protect the refugees during his absence.

His host stood and motioned for him to follow. The moment they were alone Kalau undertook to learn all he could about the village chief. What was his name? How long had he been here? Where had he come from? What was the name of his clan? Who were his parents? Remarkably the elder discovered that he and the chief were of the same clan, which meant that their bloodlines could be traced to a common ancestor.

The two men found the chief seated by a bonfire in his backyard. Elder Kalau shook his hand firmly, introduced himself, explained their blood relationship, and expressed his joy at becoming acquainted with a clan relative of such stature. The chief responded warmly.

"I need your help," Kalau began. "I and a group of friends from across the river were sitting at the mission of Kende. When trouble came there we had to leave. We are in the path to return home. We have no intention of doing anyone evil. We have been journeying on foot all day. Among us is a large group of women and small children. When we arrived a bit ago, my friend here and those living near him allowed us to sit down and gave us water to drink. While we were resting strange men came, they are threatening some among us. They have it in mind to kill people. I beg you as a blood relative to have mercy on us. Protect us from those who want to do us ill until we get across the river."

The chief shifted the discussion to other matters. After a time he told Kalau to return to the group, he would call the village elders and they would discuss the problem.

David found his people unmolested, huddled with their baggage under the open sky. Several had already fallen into exhausted sleep. He sat down on the ground with them and waited anxiously into the hours of night for word of their fate. Finally a form emerged from the darkness and called his name. He arose to respond. It was the chief.

"We have decided the matter," he said. "You can sleep in peace. I have persuaded my elders to allow you and your group to stay here tonight and to leave in the morning. I do not want the blood of friends of a kinsman on my hands."

The next morning was Monday. The fugitives ate a good meal and then made their way down the hill to the river to waiting dugout canoes. They were at the mercy of the oarsmen. Haggling was fruitless. Finally they opened their baggage and allowed the men to despoil their meager possessions as payment for ferrying the group across the river. They crossed safely. Then, on the east bank of the river, Elder Kalau gathered them around him for a worship service. "Today we give this river a new name," he said. "Truly God has brought us out of a wilderness of death and across this river into our homeland. For us, this is the river of Jordan."

Unfortunately, there were still enemies in the land. Late that afternoon the refugees arrived rain-soaked and weary at a village. They were denied any help. After dark they arrived at a second village. Begrudgingly, they were allowed shelter. The next morning, without food, they resumed their trek. They walked all day, with only brief stops for rest in the shade of scrubby roadside trees. After dark that night they trudged wearily into a village in the home area of David Kalau. Christians recognized them. They cried out with surprise, rushed to greet them, took infants from aching arms, and lifted burdens from exhausted bodies. Gratefully the weary travelers slumped on stools and mats around bonfires and relaxed among friends. It was Tuesday night — one week ago to the very hour they were enduring the holocaust of Kende station.

The next day a truck transported them to a nearby mission station. That night Pauline gave birth to her child. Students and their families returned safely to their respective home areas. For the moment at least, their ordeal had ended. But in the mind of Elder David Kalau many questions remained unanswered. Had Pastor Ilunga arrived back at Kende safely? What had happened to Pastor Lamba? What would this revolution mean for believers who could not flee as he had? When would this strife end so that people like himself, and Bertsche, and the Bible Institute students could again sit down together quietly and do the work of God?

Chapter Seven

With a steady rolling gait, Pastor Paul Lamba moved his rotund body along the slender jungle trail. He was third in a row of four men — friends — believers from his home village who were taking him to a camp of refugee Christians deep into the forest. It was midmorning. The air was heavy, moist, pungent with the odor of plant humus. At times the high canopy of overgrowth was too thick for the sun to penetrate. Then again, rays broke through the leaves to cast a lacework of shadow on the forest floor. Here the path was broken by the flaring roots of a great tree. Then it disappeared as the men traversed a carpet of dead leaves. Then it led them under a heavy low-hanging vine. Then it slipped into obscurity beneath low-growing vegetation. The atmosphere was relaxed and for the first time in many days Lamba sensed pleasure.

Such a sensation was a delightful change from the trauma of recent days. His return to visit believers and the captive missionaries at Kende Station had served a good purpose. They had welcomed him joyously. There had been no sign that they accused him of betrayal. They had hid him all day in the hospital and eventually had helped him escape into that black stormy night. They still loved him. For this knowledge he was immensely grateful.

His continuing sense of responsibility for the believers there did not allow him to flee a great distance. He had passed that night on the prairie. On the following morning he had returned to the small nearby village where the chief was his friend. Perhaps somehow this plague of terror would soon pass and he would be able to return to the station and resume his role as shepherd of the flock there. Meanwhile, Christians in the small village made him their charge.

They found trousers and a shirt for him. At that time, when he still feared greatly for his life, one of them had hidden him under a bed in a darkened corner of a hut. "I'll never let them know you are here," the believer promised as he slipped outside and closed the door; and Lamba knew the man was as good as his word. Another believer disguised himself as a rebel and returned to Kende to keep abreast of the jeunesse attitudes toward the pastor. He returned to report the area rebel commander's decree: "Don't kill Paul Lamba. Find him and bring him alive."

With the slow passing of days it became apparent that the plague of jeunesse rule would not soon end. On the contrary, Kende Station was established as a center of rebel authority. Christians no longer had reason to live there. They began filtering back to their respective home villages.

This left the pastor in a quandary. His continued presence in the nearby village jeopardized the lives of those who were hiding him. His wife and children could not join him there without betraying his presence. He hesitated returning to his own large home village. He had a house there; if the rebels pursued him in earnest, that is the first place they would search for him. Then one day these three men arrived. They offered him what seemed a reasonable alternative.

"Stop yearning for Kende Station," they counseled. "Christians have abandoned it. There is another flock looking for a shepherd. All the believers of your home village have fled to the jungle. They have built themselves a place to live near the river there to escape the harassment during these days. They want you to come and be their overseer. After you are settled there we will get your wife and children and they will join you."

So Pastor Lamba thanked the village chief and his believer friends for their hospitality and for the risks they had taken to protect him. He said goodbye and left with his three clansmen. The four men had arrived at their home village late the day before in the afternoon. Paul Lamba had gone to greet the village chief and had spent that evening conversing with him. While insurrectionists were moderately in control of the region, none had come to the village to inquire about the pastor. The chief and his people had given tacit support to the revolution from the beginning, their youth were in the movement. Believers had become increasingly restive about demands being made upon them and gradually had gone to live in the forest. The chief felt that for the present, it was important that he and the bulk of his people remain at the village. But their primary loyalty to Paul Lamba never wavered. He was one of their clansmen who had risen to a position of esteem. They would not betray him.

With this assurance Lamba wrapped an old Bible and some clothing into a small bundle and then joined his three friends on the trek into the forest. He was going to rejoin a company of believers. On occasion in years past he had been prone to complain that the work of the ministry was too costly, too demanding. How short-sighted he had been! Events he could not have foreseen had put him into a situation where he could in no way help himself and so God had sent these men to help him. Look how they were now ministering to him! What would he have done without them?

This work of caring for one another, who could put a price on it? He had no way of knowing that the most difficult lessons of caring for one another were yet to be learned. But for now, it was not simply that they wanted to repay him for past services. They valued his ministry. They wanted him to be their shepherd again. His heart became joyful.

A stick snapped and alerted him. The lead men were well ahead. He prodded himself to catch up.

During such troublesome days, what would it mean to be a shepherd of the people of Christ? A central issue was the revolution, for it was now obvious that it would not soon pass away. Christians still were looking to him for leadership. He would be compelled to take a position toward it.

At Kende he had been an outspoken opponent of the movement. Pastor James Ilunga, visiting him that night, had tried to persuade him of the folly of such a position. It appeared that the young pastor, convinced of the invincibility of the movement, had surrendered himself to it. Joining the movement did have immediate advantages. As an insider, Ilunga was able to follow its plans; he was able to anticipate its impact upon the church. Everything Ilunga had said during that night visit had come to pass! Also Ilunga's conciliatory attitude toward the revolution had blunted the rebels' wrath. Though he was beaten, he was not marked for death. He did not have to flee. He continued to circulate freely among them.

On the other hand, was it certain that the revolution would ultimately succeed? What might be the eventual consequences of openly supporting it? Maybe he should not have been so outspoken in resisting it, Lamba thought. But his conscience resisted his openly identifying himself with it. Couldn't a third position somewhere between these two be found? Perhaps it was too soon for him to formulate his position. Life or death for many people could hang upon his decision. He would wait. He would think, and watch, and pray. He did not want to make such a decision sooner than necessary.

The path broke off a forested plateau and wended its way down a long steady decline. It seemed they were approaching a river. Lamba caught the smell of wood-fire smoke.

"We are about to arrive," the man ahead of him said over a shoulder.

Soon the camp came into view. Located at the base of the hill and under the shelter of great spreading trees were two rows of huts — about fifteen in all — their walls and roofs made of large leaves tied onto stick framing in a manner which would provide adequate temporary shelter. Some were already faded and dry from exposure to the elements; others were still being constructed. On the far side of the camp a ribbon of undisturbed jungle screened the settlement from view to any traffic on the river beyond or along its opposite bank. A tiny foot trail gave refugees access to the river's water. Among the huts was a scattering of adults at work and children at play. Suddenly a few noticed the arrival of newcomers.

"Surprising affair! Who are these persons?"

"Pastor! Is that you? How are you? God be praised!"

"Our chief has arrived! Our shepherd has come!"

"Joy from heaven all the way down to earth!"

They showed him to a seat. From their limited resources they prepared a "welcome feast" for him. This warm lavish reception was the first of a sequence of happy events. The Christians cleared a space on the forest floor and helped him build a small gabled house of large leaves tied to a stick framework. Three younger men, wearing only short trousers to pass as rebels, journeyed to Kende Station. There they found Lamba's bicycle, which somehow had survived the holocaust, and his wife, Tembo, and their two children. Within a week they had left his bicycle at the last village and had brought the family to rejoin him.

Now that his immediate personal needs were provided for, Pastor Paul Lamba began to organize a ministry to the refugee families. Their food staple was manioc, an elongated starchy tuber whose plant leaves are also cooked for greens. Refugees could still frequent their fields which lay in the direction of their home village. Lamba sent men to survey outlying areas to determine the location and size of other manioc fields which could be foraged in case of emergency. By this means he determined that basic food supplies for a group of this size were adequate for a prolonged period. He took an inventory of available fishhooks. These were tied to the ends of tough freshly made raffia cord and were freely shared so that refugees had an ample supply of river fish.

These displaced villagers erected a leaf roof on four corner posts near Lamba's house. Beneath it they laid a few short posts in parallel rows on the ground for seating. They called the structure "our house of God." Early every morning Lamba conducted a worship service there. People came enthusiastically and listened intently to his teaching from the Book of God. He invited them to join him and his family at his home for regular evening prayers. They came and sat outside on the ground. In the enveloping darkness they would share their concerns, pray together, and return to their homes blessed.

None drank more deeply of these joys than did Paul Lamba. How the commitment of these people strengthened and comforted him! How precious were the strong warm bonds of family love! Like the first rains wash away the suffocating dust of a long dry season, these blessings were washing away the memories of guilt and despair. When the rebels attacked Kende that night, what if his wife had not angrily driven him into the darkness? Out on the prairie that next day, what if the voice of God had not restrained him from hanging himself? What if his three clansmen had not come in search for him? During these days thoughts of the revolution were as dark clouds receding toward the horizon, and he clung to the hope that the passing of a few months would drive them completely away.

Paul Lamba's happiness lasted for two weeks. Late one morning when he was seated at home with Tembo and their children, a friend from the village arrived. The pastor arose and greeted him.

"I have a letter for you," the messenger announced.

Lamba took the letter uncertainly, tore open the sealed envelope, and unfolded a short typed message:

SUBPOENA

Pastor Paul Lamba is to present himself at Supreme High Command Headquarters of the Revolution without delay. The purpose of his coming will be disclosed upon his arrival.

Pierre Mulele, Commander-in-Chief

Lamba froze in disbelief. A feeling of weakness wilted him. He sat down.

"What is the matter?" Tembo asked.

"I am being called."

"Who is calling you?"

He answered her without shifting his eyes from the letter. "Mulele."

The news spread like wildfire. Men dropped their work. Women swept up their infants. All came running. In a moment they circled the Lamba family, their faces etched with dismay.

"You're not going?" Tembo's face was contorted with incredulity and fear.

Their two children turned aimlessly toward the house. The nine-year-old girl pressed her brow against a forearm, went to the dried-leaf wall, leaned her arm against it, and began to weep. Her younger brother did the same.

"Where did you get this letter?" Paul asked the messenger.

"Some of our youth arrived last night with two strangers. They are waiting at the village for you."

"Who are these strangers?"

"They came from the revolution's regional headquarters. They say they are to take you to the president there."

Tembo's eyes were riveted upon him. Her incredulity gave way to despair. "Don't go! Don't go! Their plan is to kill you! They have nothing else in mind."

The pastor groped for a response. Encircling refugees waited. There was such quietness that rustling leaves sounded like thunder.

"I don't know for what purpose they are calling me," he finally said. "I am not happy to go. But now the regional president knows where I am. He has many youth under him who wait to carry out his commands. If I refuse to go, the jeunesse will come and attack our home village. They will destroy it. They will scatter the chief and all our people. It is not fair that hundreds of my clansmen suffer on account of me. On top of that, the guerrillas, if they desire to, can come here in search of me. They could add torment on top of our present suffering. I cannot stay. Why should I bring such hardship upon all of us? It is better that I go and let them do with me as they wish."

Tembo reached her arms heavenward in expression of grief and broke into sobbing.

"My God! My God! Look at my suffering! What shall I do?"

Her body convulsed uncontrollably. She began wailing as one lamenting her dead. Her children, upon seeing her grief, crumpled to the ground weeping. Women relatives clustered closely around her and began rocking to a wailing chant in an effort to comfort her.

Bystanders groped for a way to respond. Eventually a man standing near Lamba tried to wrap in words the feelings of them all.

"Pastor, our hearts are split with sadness at your leaving," he said. "Do what in your mind is right to do. But if you go, know that we are carrying you in our arms before God. We will cry with tears before Him on your behalf day and night until we see each other again."

Paul Lamba arose and went into the house. Numbed by shock, he moved insensibly, mechanically. He wrapped a clean shirt, trousers, and his Bible into a blanket, went outside, prayed a final time with his people, picked up each of his children and embraced them, firmly squeezed the shoulder of Tembo in passing through the circle of mourners, nodded at the waiting messenger, and deliberately moved toward the footpath that led up the hill. His body felt weak, his knees were as water. As he forced himself forward he heard the wail of Tembo.

"My husband! My husband! They're going to kill him!"

Chapter Eight

Stephen Kimeya stirred on his bed. He glanced toward the small bedroom window and saw the first signs of daylight. What had awakened him? Was there some kind of commotion outside? He lay quietly to listen. There was no doubt about it. He heard the sounds of muffled voices. What was going on? Perhaps neighbors had risen early. Perhaps he had heard the voices of passersby. He waited for what seemed a long time. No. These were not normal early-morning village sounds. People were waiting outside his house. Dawn had begun to lighten the room now. He eased himself from bed so as not to disturb Sona who lay beside him. Cautiously he peered through the window. The sight chilled him. He backed away and returned to the bedside. "Sona. Sona." He gently aroused her.

"What?"

"They have come to get me. Pray to God for me."

He dressed, went to the front door, sighed deeply, opened it, and walked onto the veranda. A company of about two hundred guerrillas armed with every kind of primitive weapon surrounded his house. He used their traditional greeting.

"Have you slept well?"

A few of them responded begrudgingly.

"Do you have a concern?" he asked.

"We have come hunting for you." It was the man who had been spokesman for the first rebel delegation which had visited him.

"As you see, I am here," Stephen replied calmly.

"We came to see you the first time. We asked you to give yourself to the revolution. We warned you that people were threatening your life. We wanted to take you to protect you. You said you wanted some days to think it over."

"That's right."

"After some days we came to see you again. We wanted your reply. You said that the time was not yet sufficient for you to surrender to us."

"Yes."

Some of Kimeya's neighbors emerged from their homes and stood in their yards and listened. Sona now stood in the open doorway behind him.

"Our president has sent us to get you. If you refuse to come with us willingly, we are ordered to take you by force."

Quickly Kimeya sought to size up the situation. The few weeks since the rebels' first visit had been turbulent. Mulele had sent a delegation of three men to Kimeya to investigate charges that he was hiding the mission transmitter. He proved his claim of having given it to a local tribal leader and cleared himself of the charges. A teacher originating from the Kende area headed a group of the jeunesse claiming they had orders to take him to Mulele for execution. He called their bluff and thereby foiled their plot. Chief Mazemba apparently had cast his lot with the revolution. He looted the missionaries' homes, parceling out the booty between his relatives and friends. He reasoned that he had saved the missionaries' lives, they would not be returning, and moreover the revolution had decreed that any accumulated wealth was now property of the people. Mazemba sympathized with dissident teachers who kept accusing Kimeya of crimes worthy of death. Kimeya realized that the trap was inexorably closing upon him, but he would not willingly surrender to a movement with ethics which so revolted his conscience. He steeled himself, and responded.

"Come and get me."

There was a pause of bewilderment. Then the leader gave command.

"Seize him!"

In an instant they were upon him. They pulled him off the veranda, ripped off his shirt and trousers, and threw him to the ground. They pummeled him with fists, beat him with staffs, and struck him with the broad sides of machete blades. Then they bound his hands behind him, sat him upright on the ground, and waited. Four rebels stormed through the front doorway to search the house; Sona, immobilized by shock, gazed on incredulously. They stirred through things until they were satisfied and left empty-handed. At length a truck arrived. Rebels rolled Stephen into it, climbed in until it was loaded beyond capacity, and left. The balance of the company resolutely followed on foot.

His neighbors, unprepared for such an early-morning show of violence, watched indignantly and seethed with rage.

The truck bounced six miles up the road to area command headquarters: an assortment of hastily erected huts a short distance off the road. Kimeya, dressed only in undershorts, was bruised and aching from his beating. They pushed him from the truck and conducted him to a man seated behind a table beneath a scraggly tree. The spokesman of the arresting party faced the man, stamped his bare foot at attention, and snapped a salute.

"We have come with Stephen Kimeya."

"Good," the man replied, jerking his head affirmatively. Kimeya was ordered to stand before him.

"My name is Kavua. I am zone president of the revolution. I am sorry it was necessary for my men to treat you roughly," he said with an indulgent tone. "I assure you that I do not have an evil heart toward you. Some weeks ago when you were in the path returning home, when you crossed the Loange River, I and my men were watching you. I told them, 'Let him pass; we don't need to harm him.' "

The words did little to assuage Stephen's pain.

"The first time my men came to visit you, they informed you that many people were accusing you of many things. They explained to you that your life was in danger. Right up to now the accusations keep multiplying. Your enemies say you are a criminal. They demand that you be executed. They keep stirring up people to join them. When I saw these things happening, I had compassion on you. I sent my men to get you. By doing this I am saving your life. Moreover, people will see that you cannot do the things they accuse you of and will settle down. I have done you well, have I not? Now, if you please, be happy to stay here with me and to follow my instructions."

Kimeya gazed at Kavua expressionlessly. He would thank the rebel leader for nothing. Why should a man be complimented for assault and subterfuge?

"Untie his hands," Kavua ordered. "Show him to a hut where he can stay and keep a sharp eye on him."

They furnished Kimeya his minimal needs. During the day they allowed him liberty within the confines of the camp. Just over a week passed and furor over his arrest subsided. Then one morning Kimeya's father Kapala arrived at the camp to visit him. Guards reported Kapala's arrival to President Kavua. The rebel leader may have turned away others seeking to visit Kimeya. But he had publicly professed compassion for Kimeya. Denying his prisoner such a basic privilege would be embarrassing. Also such denial could dangerously inflame the feelings of the Mudidi people. Kavua ordered that Kapala be shown to Kimeya's hut.

Kapala was a tall slender man in his fifties, a seasoned age by African standards. He had been a Christian since childhood. He learned early the principles of honesty, hard work, and responsibility, and had sought to inculcate them into his son. An elder in the church on Mudidi station, he was respected as a man with resources to get things done.

Stephen was immensely heartened by his father's visit. The two were very close. It was the first of many visits. Kapala brought notes from Sona. He kept Stephen informed of ongoing relationships between the people of Chief Mazemba and leaders of the revolution. Initially most people were cooperative. Mulele sent a warning that American planes would come to bomb the station; people should cut down palm branches and cover metal roofs with them as a camouflage. The people complied. Then he sent word that personal valuables should be buried in the ground so that they would be protected in case of an attack. Again the people complied. A few days later they discovered that their valuables had been disinterred and stolen.

Seeds of resentment began to sprout. Church

leaders were annoyed by the apparent efforts of rebel leaders to control activities on Mudidi station. Then Chief Mazemba and his elders became irked by what appeared to be efforts to flout their tribal authority. For purposes of administration, the rebel leadership had grouped the people under Mazemba's jurisdiction with diverse larger population blocks which had a long history of strained relations with them. The people of Mazemba were thereby reduced to a voiceless minority. Revolution leaders had planted this "Zone Command Headquarters" on Mudidi's doorstep and had placed Kavua, an immigrant from an unrenowned tribe, in charge. Mazemba's people fumed over Kavua's efforts to control them. Kimeya's alienation from Chief Mazemba made it impossible for him to lend his influence to the situation. However, he regularly relayed his counsel through his father to station church leaders to quietly and resolutely continue their normal activities.

Stephen was in captivity for about a month when Kapala brought a note from Sona saying she was pregnant. Kapala also brought word of a mounting crisis.

"The revolution leaders are angry at the stubbornness of leaders on Mudidi station. They have vowed to break our rebelling against them," he reported.

"What are they doing?"

"They want to stop our work of helping people."

"How?"

"For example, there is our medical work. When the jeunesse attacked centers of government authority they chased out workers in charge of dispensaries and purloined the medicines. The revolution has been promising people good things. Now it cannot alleviate their illnesses. So rebel leaders keep trying to take control of the hospital on Mudidi station. They are like people who, after having already eaten a whole chicken, pick a fuss with the dog for eating the chicken's head."

"What is their strategy?"

"They keep sending letters to the director of the hospital demanding that he send them reports on this and that. They send him their counsel on how he should change his way of doing things. They know not the tiniest thing about running a hospital."

"How is the director of the hospital responding to this?"

"He refuses to send them reports. He and his workers aren't changing a thing. They are offended that these outsiders having arrived today, order them, as experienced people, how to do things."

"Good," Stephen affirmed. "Tell them to strengthen their hearts."

"The rebel leaders also are trying to rule the church."

"In what way?"

"One day we received word that it was all right for us to keep going to church, but the services should not last so long and we should finish quickly so people could get back to their work. Some days passed. Then we were sent word that it was not good to ring the church bell or to beat the calling drum; the noise annoyed people who were not interested in the services."

"Are church leaders complying?"

"No. They resent being given such laws. They say they will persevere in worshiping God the way the missionaries always taught them."

"How do Mazemba's village people feel about these affairs?"

"They back up the station leaders. They are proud of our hospital and of our church. They say they will resist this kind of arrogancy until frogs sprout feathers. That is why the revolutionary leaders are so angry. The people of Mudidi are like a palm nut in their throat. They cannot tolerate this kind of insubordination. Now they are saying, 'Because you refuse to work with us in forwarding the revolution, you are a threat to peace. Lock up the hospital. Lock up the church. If you don't, you are hunting trouble.' "

"Lock them up?" Stephen felt the heat of anger. "For what reason? How will people get help with their sicknesses? Where are they to worship?"

"Do you see that these revolution leaders in their hearts want to help people?" Kapala rejoined. "Not a bit. All they want is to climb into their chairs of chieftainship and make the earth's progeny bow at their feet. When I see all these affairs, I wonder what the end of it all will be."

"Their plans are designed to make people suffer!" Stephen's eyes flashed his displeasure. "Such wisdom isn't coming from God. It comes from Satan. Tell the church fathers to plug their ears to such words. Tell them to stick to obeying the Word of God. Let us leave the end of all this in the hands of the Creator."

President Kavua, Zone Commander of the revolution, was perplexed as to how to deal with the intransigence of Chief Mudidi and his people. The leader sat with half a dozen subordinates in his hut and asked their counsel.

"In all other places these tactics have caused people to submit to us. Why does that village of Mudidi persevere in its stubbornness?"

There was an appropriate pause to solicit the commander's respect.

"I respond with a proverb of the ancestors," replied one rebel. "They said, 'It isn't the ill-smelling herb in the distant valley that is deranging the people; it is the sorcerer who lives next to you.' "

"Explain what you mean."

"The one who feeds the stubbornness of the Mudidi people is no one a distance away. It is their clansman Kimeya who is living here with us."

"That's right!" affirmed another. "You had him arrested and brought here so that he could no longer do his work. You hoped he would begin to help us. But since he arrived, do you see that he has changed his heart? Not a bit. It is he who is giving the people of Mudidi hard ears. He sends instructions to them with his father Kapala. Have you ever seen a torch weaken a fire? The stubbornness of those people will not weaken until you remove Kimeya."

The others nodded in agreement.

"What shall we do with him?" Kavua asked.

"In spite of your showing him mercy, he doesn't respect you," affirmed another. "He doesn't fear you. He persists in obstructing the revolution. What do the laws of the movement instruct us to do with such a person? Do they not tell us to eliminate him?"

The Zone Commander responded cautiously. "The people of Mudidi greatly respect Kimeya. If he were destroyed, what would happen? It would start war. If they attacked us, could we repulse them? No. We have not yet prepared ourselves for that. But I agree that Kimeya must be separated from his people. I'll send him away — far away. I will send him to a place where he will either help the revolution or be eliminated."

One morning Kimeya was called to report to Kavua.

"You have sat quietly with us," the commander said ingratiatingly. "I don't see that you've caused us any trouble. But you are a man of wisdom. You have many skills. This is a small post. I have no way of making good use of you. I am sending you to the commander-in-chief of the revolution, Pierre Mulele. He will make good use of your gifts. Also, he will be able to decide whether accusations people are making against you are true or false. I am sending you with four armed men; they will see that you arrive safely. Food is being prepared now. After you eat you will go."

Chapter Nine

Over two weeks had passed since the rebel leaders had called Pastor Paul Lamba from his forest hideaway. The incident made clear that the insurrectionists knew the location of the refugee camp, it no longer offered a haven from rebel harassment. Consequently most believers who had taken refuge there returned to join clansmen in their home villages.

Such was the case with Lamba's wife Tembo. As is the custom when a family member dies, relatives and close friends came to her home daily and sat with her to offer their solace. Late one afternoon Tembo was sitting with a cluster of women on the floor on her earth-walled thatch-roofed home. They sat in a rear room which opened onto the backyard. Across the door threshold in the yard men sat on chairs in a small circle. Suddenly there was the familiar thump of a bicycle being placed against a front veranda post. Then came jubilant shouts.

"Keeeeya! Pastor!"

"Are our eyes deceiving us?"

"Lamba! Is that you?"

"It is he! It is he! Who else?"

"Affair of surprise! Joy from heaven to earth!"

"Our kinsman was dead; he has returned to life again!"

Suddenly Paul Lamba was there; standing in the doorway. He crossed the threshold. His children rushed to embrace him. Tembo stared at him, then collapsed at his feet. He squatted to comfort her.

African hospitality demands that hosts fill a newcomer's stomach before they ask him to unburden his heart. The pastor ate well that night. Then he was shown to a chair at an outside bonfire and village people packed themselves around him as thick as blades of grass to hear his story.

"Clansmen, I tell you that had God not been with me, I wouldn't be with you tonight," the pastor affirmed. "We were in the path four days to arrive at the camp of Mulele. His place is deep in the forest. When he saw me and learned my name he said, 'Ahhhh — the pastor from Kende. He is the one who is giving people hard heads and exciting them to overthrow me. Sit down there.' I sat down on the ground in front of him. I knew I was in trouble.

"At that time, about fifty feet from me, they were killing a man. Youths, male and female, were pounding him with clubs. He was moaning and writhing. I began weeping. I told myself, 'When they finish killing him they'll come get me to kill me too.' Fear caught me. Sweat began

112

running down my body in rivers. I bowed my head and wailed to God. I told Him I was His child, I was innocent. Why was this happening to me? When I stopped praying and looked up — what a surprising thing — I saw that Mulele's helper, the one who sits on his right hand, was a person I knew."

"His name is Kalugu. Once when traveling far away, I was invited to stay at his home overnight. Friendship caught us. Whenever I journeyed in that direction I stayed at his house. Another time when he was traveling, he came and stayed with me. Kalugu interceded for me before Mulele. When Mulele saw how afraid I was, and after he heard the words of Kalugu, he laughed. He said, 'We aren't going to kill you, pastor. We just want to keep you here.' Look how God responded to my wailing! It is good to make friends with whomever you meet. Another time, that friendship may save you. Look at me now! That's why I'm here!"

Pastor Lamba described Pierre Mulele: egotistical, unyielding, temperamental. He described the camp: its structure, its people, its daily activities. He told how Kalugu eventually convinced Mulele of Lamba's integrity; this led to an unexpected assignment.

"On my eighth day there," Paul recalled, "Mulele told me that I would be returning home. I rejoiced surpassingly. He said, 'You have the gift of teaching. I want you to help me. The revolution is succeeding. But some of the youth are going crazy. They are not following my instructions. They are torturing and pillaging wantonly. As you go, teach people that it is not good to torment fathers and mothers and compatriots pointlessly. They are to respect one another and to sit in their villages at peace.'

"These words amazed me exceedingly. I asked him if I could teach the Word of God. He said, 'Yes, it is good to teach the affair of God. Our forefathers believed in God. I have not renounced God. When you get home, sit quietly among your clansmen and persevere in teaching them these things.' Then he told a secretary to prepare a path paper for me. Here it is." Lamba drew it from a shirt pocket and unfolded it. "It has my name on it. It gives me authority to teach people. It says anyone harassing me or the people under my charge are to be arrested and taken to Mulele. See: there is his signature. For all these things I glorify God. When they came and called me from the forest, Christians began praying for me. Look how God has answered their prayers!"

Late that night people went to their huts marveling. Suddenly their clansman Paul Lamba was a man of extraordinary esteem. He had socialized with the commander-in-chief. In his pocket was a paper. That paper carried the authority of Mulele himself.

Pastor Paul Lamba also had been somewhat swept off his feet by the recent rush of events. When Tembo finally rolled over to go to sleep,

Lamba began mentally to try and sort things out. The Bible says that all good things come from God. Lamba was alive and back home. Surely that was good. For that he praised God. But what were the real implications of his new stature with Mulele? What did this say about his relation to the revolution?

Lamba had been selective about what he had shared with the village people that evening. Mulele also had said that the only people who must be killed are those who refuse to submit to his authority. Mulele wanted Lamba to help him win the trust of the people so that they would sit quietly under his rule and support what he was doing. While Mulele had encouraged Lamba to "teach the affair of God," he had insisted that missionaries had deceived people on some matters and were not to be recalled. Lamba had not mentioned these things this evening. He did not want to imply that he condoned killing, or that he had accepted to be a political emissary for Mulele, or that he agreed with Mulele's opinion of the missionaries.

Unilaterally Mulele had entrusted Lamba with a duty. Lamba's release was based on Mulele's assumption that Lamba would faithfully discharge that duty. Had Lamba been dishonest in accepting release and thereby implying such loyalty? He abhorred the violence of the movement. Some parts of Mulele's assignment he could with good conscience discharge. Others he could not.

What about the path paper given him by
Mulele? During his journey home it had already
swiftly deflected the harassment of the jeunesse
bands. Does a legal paper of a government in
power mean that its holder endorses all that the
government does? No. Paul decided he would
continue to use it. Nonetheless, he recognized
that possession of the paper tacitly implied his
endorsement of the Mulelist regime.

Lamba recalled the words of James Ilunga:
anyone standing against the revolution would be
crushed like a butterfly beneath a tumbling
boulder. While in custody at Mulele's camp
Lamba had seen that crushing in process. He remembered those last days at Kende when he
spoke out loudly against the revolution. But for
God's mercy, he too would have been clubbed to
death. In accepting Mulele's assignment that he
go and teach, he had implied a loyalty to the revolution which was not genuine. While his conscience would not allow him to openly support
the movement, it was apparent that he was now
compromising with it.

Was such a position wrong? It appeared that
events of recent days had decreed it. What could
he have done to make things come out differ-
ently? Mulele had made it clear that there was
one end for those who resisted him: death.
Should Lamba have violated their tradition of
accepting hospitality by scorning the generosity
of his friend Kalugu? He thereby would have
sealed his own doom. Then how could Chris-

116

tians who had been praying for him day and night say that God had answered their prayers? Compromise was dangerous. He felt like a man trying to cross a river on a slippery log. Would he reach the other shore? He must try. Now that he had begun this course, he felt that there was no turning back. He would have to pursue it. From the time these troubles had started God had watched over him in an amazing way; surely God could be trusted to care for him into the future.

Paul Lamba's position was soon tested. One day Pastor James Ilunga came to visit him and spelled out for him the implications of his new-found friendship with Mulele.

"Government soldiers are trying hard to find Mulele. When they learn that you have been to his camp, they will be searching for you," Ilunga warned him. "If you refuse to tell them where Mulele sits, they'll torment you until they find out. If soldiers learn that Mulele has given you a document authorizing you to be his teacher, they will see you as a promoter of the revolution. This makes you their enemy. They have not the tiniest bit of love for their enemies. They kill them. When you sit here, not only are you in danger. You are endangering your wife and your children and all your clansmen who live here with you. In the days that are ahead government soldiers will try hard to recover this area. It is not good for you to sit here. I beg of you to come with Tembo and your children to sit where we are."

James Ilunga described in detail their distant

hideaway. It was in forested hills surrounded by two battalions of well-armed guerrillas; they were well protected. They had taken custody of the cattle of a large ranching enterprise now abandoned and they had plenty to eat.

"Now that the Kazavubu government sees you as its enemy, if you want to stay alive, you should give yourself to the revolution," the young pastor reasoned. "Moreover, I need your help. Some of the jeunesse no longer respect leadership of the movement; they are causing innocent people to suffer. You can help me intercede on behalf of those who are suffering pointlessly. Have you heard how I interceded for the Bible Institute families? I saved their lives and helped them return to their homeland safely! If you and I worked together, we could comfort many people; we could bring the foolish thinking of the jeunesse back into the right path and we could help pacify the land."

It was late at night when they finished talking. James Ilunga went to sleep at another home in the village. Paul Lamba arranged it that way. He wanted to have ample opportunity to discuss Ilunga's proposal with Tembo. Her answer was clear.

"I'll oppose that kind of thinking perpetually," she exclaimed. "When they took you to see Mulele, my children and I never expected to see you alive again. When you were gone, you don't know how the Christians pleaded with God for you! How they supported us! God has returned

118

you to us alive. These believers love us. These people are our clansmen. Are they afraid now because you are here? No. They are rejoicing. You are their hero. Now you are thinking that we should leave them? For what reason? I know that Ilunga has done some good things because of his friendship with the rebels. But do you remember those days before Kende was burned? Ilunga had the custom of frequenting drinking places where men sit all day holding their heads. Doesn't the Bible say that God will bless those who refuse to stand in the path with evildoers or sit at one place with the scornful? In my thinking, we are staying here with our relatives in Christ and with our clansmen. Death and life are in the hands of God. The day He says we die, we die."

Paul Lamba agreed with her. It was true that government forces might be searching for him. If they caught him, he could well suffer. On the other hand, he was not at all sure that the revolution was succeeding. If the government army gained the offensive and eventually crushed the movement, few of the revolution's ardent supporters were likely to escape alive. The risks of accepting Ilunga's counsel were too great. For the sake of his conscience and of survival, he did not want to cast his lot with the movement's ardent supporters. Still, he had an unnerving reminiscence. He recalled another visit by Pastor James Ilunga: hours before Kende was attacked. He had spurned James' counsel then and later had found himself in deep trouble. Nonetheless, next morning he called Ilunga, tactfully explained why he felt he must decline the young pastor's proposal, and bade him fare-well.

About ten days later there was an omen that Ilunga's prophecy might come true. One midafternoon two armed government soldiers arrived, casually conversed with a few village people along the roadside, and moved on. In all probability they were advance scouts for a mili-tary attack force. That evening the chief called a meeting of his village elders and Lamba. A dozen men gathered around a bonfire at the chief's house to discuss the incident.

"We must accept that soon the government army will arrive," the chief stated. "The question we must decide is this: what thinking will the sol-diers take toward us? Will they deal with us as enemies or will they greet us as friends?"

"Can government soldiers be pleased with us?" one elder deliberated. "They know that many of our youth have entered the movement. Whenever guerrillas come here asking for some-thing to eat, we feed them. Why should the gov-ernment soldiers count us their friends?"

"Perhaps soldiers know about the trip of Pastor Lamba," said another. "Those two who were here today, what did they come for? Per-haps to spy on him. How can we know?"

"Lamba has a letter which protects us from harassment by the jeunesse, but who has a letter to protect us from harassment by the military?" mused a third.

The group decided that the approaching government forces posed an imminent threat to the safety of the people of the village.

"When things are like this, what do you think we should do?" the chief asked.

"Let's remember the words of our ancestors: 'Chicken, when you see the knife and pot, decide for yourself what to do,' " reminded a wrinkled old man. "If we want to live, we will flee. We will go hide in the forest."

Others added concurring remarks. There was a long pause as the council weighed the implications of such a plan.

"Are you saying that everybody should go live in the forest whether or not he wants to?" one demurred.

"We aren't going to live in the forest because we want to," the chief reminded. "We are going there to save our lives. Suppose soldiers came and discovered one person at his house. What would happen?"

"They would catch him and interrogate him."

"That's right. They would force him to betray the whereabouts of us all."

"Then we would all really suffer."

It was agreed to vacate the village.

"How long will we sit in the forest?" one queried.

"We will sit there until the soldiers of Kazavubu and the guerrillas of Mulele finish disputing over who is to rule our land," the chief stated. "That may be a long time. A wise man gathers his palm wine before the storm. If we want to do what is right, we will begin moving to the forest tomorrow morning. We are fortunate. No one is forcing us to flee empty-handed. We can take with us whatever we think we will need to reduce our discomfort. Though a hen has no breasts, it feeds its biddies. If we work hard and perseveringly, we and our children will survive. Is this what we should do?"

Men around the circle nodded and grunted affirmatively.

"What other path is left for us to follow?"

"That is what we must do."

"Then go spread the news to every home," the chief ordered. "People need to prepare themselves."

Dawn the next morning brought with it feverish activity. Men, machetes in hand, went to the forest hideaway where believers had formerly taken refuge and began preparing shelters. Women and older children began arduous shuttling trips to transport their personal effects from their village homes into the forest. Within a week the village site was deserted. The jungle camp perimeter formerly enclosed living space for a population of about forty, now it stretched to accommodate almost five hundred.

Pastor Paul Lamba and his family repaired their stick and leaf house and reoccupied it. Then one afternoon he received word that the chief was calling him. He went and found the chief sitting in council with his elders. They greeted him and motioned toward an empty stool that was waiting for him. He sat down.

"The burden of caring for our people is greater now because we are sitting in the forest," the chief began. "You are a renowned person among us. We need your help."

"What kind of help?" the pastor asked.

"My village elders and I will continue to judge disputes between persons," he explained. "We will make important decisions like what to do or where to go in case trouble catches us. But an important matter we have here is that of food. The Christians tell us that when you were with them here you took good care of them. None of them failed what they needed to remain in health. Now that we are all of us here together, we want you to take up that work again. We want you to be caretaker of the refugees to see that they sit well and have what they need."

"It isn't only that you have already done this work of feeding people," an elder at the chief's right hand continued before Lamba could protest. "You alone have seen Mulele face-to-face. You have a letter from him which will restrain rebels from harassing us. We have seen that no one else is qualified for this work like you."

Lamba pondered the import of their words. "You are giving me a heavy burden," he said.

"We will work together with you," the chief declared. "The hunter never carries an elephant

123

carcass home alone. His people must say, 'It is the burden of us all.' "

"It is not an easy matter for me to accept your request," the pastor replied. "But if you agree to help me, I cannot refuse it. You must promise me that we will be one in this matter, working together like the fingers of a hand."

"We are one with you," the elders affirmed, nodding their heads vigorously.

Paul Lamba rose and slowly left for home. His new responsibility gave him at once a sense of awe and of fear.

"My God," he prayed. "Where will we find food enough for all these people? For how long will we need to feed them?"

Chapter Ten

It was early June of 1964. Stephen Kimeya, still clad only in undershorts, stumbled wearily from a dark forest path into the sunlight. He and four guards were terminating a harrowing five-day foot journey. En route they had encountered a truckload of armed soldiers. Fleeing ensuing gunfire, they had barely escaped with their lives. For the last day and a half they had coursed their way through seemingly impenetrable jungle to reach their destination. Now he stood on the edge of a vast open space where rank undergrowth had been cleared and huts had been built beneath a diffusion of towering trees. He had arrived at the hideaway headquarters of Pierre Mulele, commander-in-chief of the revolution.

Kimeya's eyes scanned the scene. Four long straight rows of huts formed the four sides of a square enclosing the camp. Three larger houses dominated its center. Toward the far end of the square beneath a tree a man was lecturing a group of about thirty rebels seated on the ground before him. Stephen followed his escort toward one of the larger houses where a man a bit older than he was seated behind a worn table. The house was to the man's right. To his left was a long, shedlike structure with a one-way roof. Through its high, open front one could see secretaries busy at typewriters.

The man at the table was dressed in khaki: shorts, an unbuttoned shirt, and a two-corner military "overseas" cap. Stephen fastened his attention upon the man. Muscles in his smooth lean face were taut; his frame was spare and sinewy. He was tense, like an animal poised to spring. One of Kimeya's guards took a position in front of the man, stamped his right foot on the ground, snapped a salute, gave his report, and stepped to one side. Stephen Kimeya was nudged into the guard's position. He stood before the man whom he now knew to be Pierre Mulele.

"Hmmmmm — so you are that big friend of the Americans from Mudidi?" Mulele observed. "I've been told about you. Now that the Americans are gone, I hear you are still giving people hard heads to resist the revolution."

"I have never entered into the squabblings of you politicians," Stephen replied. "I was sitting quietly at home until your people came and took me by force."

"What were you keeping in your home? When your American friends departed they didn't leave you with empty hands. The transmitter you were using — did you bring it with you?"

"I already proved to your people that I no

longer have the transmitter. Your jeunesse searched my house. They found neither a transmitter nor the other things they accused me of concealing."

"Kavungu," Mulele announced to a husky-framed man standing on his right hand, "take this man away. Give him food and a place to sleep. We will take up his case again tomorrow."

Kimeya's hunger and fatigue from the long journey subdued his anxiety. He ate and was shown to a mat on an earthen hut floor where he slept. Midmorning the next day Kavungu called him to go stand before Mulele.

"Do you see these letters?" the rebel commander asked, his thumb flipping through the corner of a stack of papers an inch high. "These letters were written by people who know you. They accuse you of many things: you helped the missionaries escape, you are a friend of the Kazavubu government, you inform it of our activities, and you counsel people against joining us and so obstruct the revolution. If a court of Kazavubu were trying you, you would not have a chance. His judges would take bribes from your accusers and then condemn you. The tribunals of the revolution are just. I reprimand an offender two or three times. If he refuses to change his ways, then I condemn him. I want to keep you here until I understand your case clearly. Take these letters. Read them for yourself. See if those who have written them are persons you know. If some have been written by strangers, tell me.

When the time is sufficient, we will talk about whether or not these accusations are true. I have nothing else to say to you now. Kavungu," he announced to his right-hand man, "have you finished preparing his place?"

The man nodded.

"Take him there."

Kavungu took him to a windowless hut made of large, dry leaves tied to a sturdy stick framework about thirty yards away. A guard named "Kipoko" ordered him to enter it, closed the door behind him, and locked it. The hut's only furnishings were a straight chair and a reed sleeping mat unrolled on its floor. Suddenly Kimeya realized that he was imprisoned — in solitary confinement.

His head was swimming. He sat on the chair to try and gather his thoughts. What did this incarceration mean? Did Mulele sincerely want to give him a fair trial? Or were the rebel commander's smooth words meant to disguise covert plans to destroy him? How were the people of Mudidi responding to his deportation? How were his wife, Sona, and the children enduring the trauma of his arrest and his prolonged absence? How could he possibly disentangle himself from his present predicament? Would he ever see those he loved on earth again?

"If my Father in heaven still cares about me," the prisoner mused, "what good thing could He possibly have in mind to bring out of all this?"

At length he decided that for the moment he

could only assume that Mulele was sincere. He spent the day reading the letters one by one. In effect, teachers whom he had once supervised before the turmoil had begun were now double-crossing him to demonstrate their unadulterated allegiance to the revolution. Shortly after noon someone brought him an aluminum plate with manioc mush and greens. He ate. By midafternoon he needed to urinate. He called through a crack between the door and its crude casement to Kipoko, his guard, who stood nearby. The guard escorted him to a partially covered privy hole, watched him, then put him back into his hut and locked the door.

Time passed slowly day after day. Kimeya virtually memorized the accusing letters. Then, by peeping through cracks in his prison walls, he became familiar with his surroundings. Mulele spent most of his time seated behind his table: he gave orders to his secretaries, signed their letters, sent messengers, received delegations, judged those accused of crimes against the revolution. The larger house to Mulele's left was his residence. The other two houses in the center of the camp belonged to Kavungu whose title was "military chief," and to a man who was called "political chief." Various smaller huts nearby provided storage for confiscated property the rebels brought from their raiding forays — private property which now belonged to "the people."

Female partisans slept in the three center houses. Male rebels slept in the four rows of huts which formed the camp perimeter. Those living in each row constituted a "company", and in a hut midway along each row lived a "company commander." Obviously the camp layout was strategic, in case of military attack from any quarter, rebel trainees could defend the camp and their leaders.

Kimeya soon perceived a daily routine of camp activities. First came reveille. Trainees were aroused by a sentry pounding a piece of iron on a scrap brake drum suspended from a tree limb. They lined up by companies. Their commanders took roll and in turn reported to Military Chief Kavungu who was in charge. Then came roll call of the guards who had been on duty the previous night. They reported any significant happenings. Guard supervisors would report any guards caught delinquent in their duties of the past night; forthwith, delinquents were laid on the ground and a team of trainees under command flogged them mercilessly.

After roll call Kavungu conducted an hour of military instruction. First came gymnastics. Trainees animated themselves by boisterously chanting slogans of loyalty to Mulele and to the revolution. Then Kavungu drilled them in the use of hand weapons. Finally he taught them combat strategies. Kimeya strained his ears to hear this instruction. It helped explain the rebels' reputation of invincibility.

"When you want to attack your enemies," Stephen heard the military chief say, "choose a place where they will come over a hill and down the slope toward you. Keep them on higher ground above you. That way they will expose themselves, and you stay concealed. Before the battle, know the place where you will be fighting like you know the hair on your arm. Come to agreement on how you are going to start fighting and what each group is going to do. Make a second plan to follow if the first one should not succeed. And know what paths to follow if you must retreat into the valley. When you retreat, don't run straight away. Always run zigzagging so that bullets of those chasing you will miss you."

"You know enemy soldiers will be coming down such-and-such a road," Kavunga said another time. "Where it passes through the forest, dig a deep pit across it. Cover the hole with sticks and camouflage it with sand. A sufficient number of fighters should surround the place, hiding some distance away. Three or four of them with guns should stand behind large trees closer to the road. About forty yards beyond the pit, two guerrillas should hide along the edge of the road; a third one should hide himself high in a tree near them as a sentry. When the sentry sees the truck loaded with soldiers coming, just before it reaches the pit he whistles to the two men; they run out into the road for a tiny moment to reveal themselves, and then flee into the forest. They do this only to catch the eyes of the soldiers just before the front wheels of the truck fall into the pit. Then the truck hits the pit, throwing soldiers this way and that. One of the guerrillas hiding behind a tree shoots. Then another on the other side of the road shoots. Now the hearts of the soldiers have split with fear. They think guerrillas fill the forest around them. They begin shooting everywhere. When they stop shooting, another guerrilla hiding behind a tree shoots and starts them again. By this means the soldiers will waste all their ammunition. When their shooting is finished, comrades waiting in the circle can close in to trap the soldiers. Using the weapons of our forefathers, they can kill them all."

After the period of military instruction and a recess, the political chief lectured trainees on the ideology of the movement. A capitalist regime always causes great inequality of wealth. The revolution would eliminate oppression and poverty by sharing wealth with everyone equally. Kimeya had heard it so often that the man's daily lecturing reminded him of the monotonous squawking of a parrot. Following the lecture, trainees were divided into work details. After the noon meal, the morning schedule was repeated, terminating in the late afternoon when trainees were allowed free time until supper. Evenings were spent in revelry: drinking, dancing, and singing to the accompaniment of drums and a battered guitar.

What Stephen saw and heard through the course of each succeeding day gave him little reason to hope that he would ever be set free. His skimpy meal a day left him always hungry. He felt abandoned. His fate hung on the mercurial Mulele who one moment was complaisantly kind and the next moment was hurling thunderbolts of rage. The commander's judgment was severe, particularly upon those whom he felt were guilty of collaborating with the central government. Kimeya had worked for the mission. That is what got him into all this trouble. He vowed that if he ever got out of this place, he would never work for the mission again.

Kimeya completed a week in prison. Relaxed security allowed him to have an occasional visitor. Two of them were Christian clansmen originating from Mudidi. One brought him a pair of trousers and another brought him a Bible sent to him by his parents; it was concealed in dirty wrapping paper. Visitors' testimonies confirmed Kimeya's suspicions about forms of punishment Mulele meted out to the guilty.

"When a person is sentenced to death," they informed Stephen, "his pants legs are ripped off to mark him as condemned. If he is to remain alive overnight, he is thrown into a hole in the ground. The hole is not large enough for persons in it to lie down or to stand; they can only sit with heads and shoulders stooped. Then the pit is covered with heavy logs and dirt for the night so that people outside will not be annoyed by the prisoner's yelling. Sometimes they kill a person by cutting off his head. Other times the jeunesse, males and females working together, tie a person's ankles, wrists, and neck with a rope, pulling his feet and head together behind him until he is rolled into a round bundle. Then they club him to death. Other times they will bury a person alive; after he is covered, noises such as you have never heard come from the ground until he is dead."

While at Mudidi, Stephen Kimeya had decided that he must resist the revolution. What he was witnessing now only hardened his resolve. He, a Christian since childhood, could never willingly be part of such sadism and violence. Rebels held him at their mercy. They were no friends of the Book of God. He began reading his Bible surreptitiously. It brought him comfort and hope like a shaft of light breaking through the darkness. He found his attention drawn repeatedly to the Macedonian call of the Apostle Paul (Acts 16:9). Was this the work of the Holy Spirit? Where was God calling him to? Was God telling him this was not the end — that there was still work for him to do?

During his second week in prison, the growing pain of his isolation and hunger seemed unbearable. His Bible reading gave him courage to make a desperate decision. He would risk provoking confrontation in an effort to improve his lot. What was the difference if he died of neglect in prison or from an effort to change things.

He began reading his Bible boldly. Partisans reported the activity. Mulele refused to make an issue of it. Kimeya thanked God and thereafter studied the book unhindered. He began insisting that his guard Kipoko carry his appeal to Mulele to examine his case. Finally, Kipoko brought him word that Mulele was still trying to establish the truth or falsehood of accusations against him. By the end of his second week in prison, what he had read in the Scriptures encouraged him to risk confrontation. Then unexpectedly his decision was put to a test.

One morning he thought he heard familiar voices. He listened intently. He couldn't believe his ears. He heard the voices of mission friends he had worked with through the years. At first he feared hallucinations. He listened intently. Missionaries and African leaders were discussing business on one of their daily broadcasts, just as he had done many times. He peeked outside and saw the rebels clustered around a radio. Holding his breath, he heard the call letters and messages of each station in turn. He linked each succeeding voice immediately with a familiar face. Then he heard the call letters of Kikwit, the provincial capital, and the voice of a veteran missionary, a co-laborer with him in the mission's educational program. Involuntarily a rush of warm memories flooded his mind, then dashed themselves against the awareness of his immediate predicament. The effect was as if someone had stabbed him in the abdomen and were twisting the knife.

Suddenly, a powerful local signal blasted

through the speaker; a voice was lauding the cause of the revolution. It was clear now: the rebels had brought a confiscated transceiver and battery to the camp and were broadcasting propaganda messages on the frequency used for mission broadcasts.

Kimeya was overcome with emotion. He slumped forward on his chair and held his head in his hands. He wept for a while. Tears coursed freely. Then slowly he began to grasp the implications of this unexpected development. A plan began to form in his mind. Mulele insisted that he was looking for evidence to prove the truth or falsehood of accusations against his prisoner from Mudidi. Now Kimeya devised a means which would at once test Mulele's sincerity and provide him with that evidence. Stephen filled in details of the scheme. He recognized that it was fraught with danger. But it also held hope. He screwed up courage and determined to take the risk.

"Kipoko! Kipoko! Come here," he called.

"Stop your noise!" the guard replied. "Don't you know that your noise may annoy Mulele? He will make me beat you." The guard was approaching the hut door.

"I'm not bothering you for nothing," Stephen explained. "I want you to take me to Mulele. I want to see him today."

"Why do you want to see Mulele?"

"He keeps telling me that he is trying to establish whether accusations against me are true or false. If he wishes, I will prove to him that they are false."

"Why does this require that you see him today? He has many visitors today. I'll tell him about it tomorrow morning."

"During all these days you have been guarding me, have I troubled you one time with such a request? Now today when I ask you, you answer, 'I'll look into that business tomorrow.' Mulele says the revolution is to serve the people. He wants to hear about their sufferings. How is it that he has time to hear the troubles of all these visitors, but you don't want him to listen to the troubles of somebody who is living with him every day? The forefathers said, 'Why do you keep feeding strangers while your children starve?' Does the revolution despise the wisdom of our forefathers?"

"Stop coercing me. I'll go tell him. But what if he refuses to see you?"

"Tell him the words I just told you. He'll not refuse to see me. If he does, I'll keep on aggravating you until he accepts to see me, even if you beat me."

Apparently Kipoko delivered the message correctly. Stephen Kimeya was escorted into the presence of Pierre Mulele.

"What is bothering you?" the commander-in-chief asked brusquely.

"My request is not without purpose," the prisoner replied. "I think I can help you solve your problem with me. I am happy to recall your promise to me the day I arrived. You said that the government of the revolution pursues justice. You said you wanted to keep me here until you understood my case clearly. You said you are still waiting for evidence which would show whether the accusations against me are true or false."

"That is correct."

"In many of the letters you gave me to read, teachers accuse me of having embezzled their salary moneys. If I proved to you that I never received those salary moneys, what would you say about those teachers?"

"I would say that they are accusing you falsely."

"Chief, I beg of you, when the mission stations are broadcasting tomorrow morning, accept for me to transmit a message. I will talk to a missionary on the radio who will give you the evidence you are searching."

Mulele eyed the prisoner suspiciously, furrowing his brows in thought. Finally he answered.

"I have heard your words. You are not asking a light thing. I need to discuss the matter with others. I will give you my answer before the sun sets."

Kimeya returned to the hut, his heart pounding. Fear was mixed with expectation. He spent the time pleading to God in prayer. Near sundown Mulele called him.

"You count on me as being a man of honesty,"

the rebel commander said. "I also count on you as being a man of honesty. I trust that your request is sincere and is not a ruse to betray us. You may talk with the missionary tomorrow morning, but I am sending sixty men with guns to watch you. If the missionary asks questions designed to trap you, you will remain silent. In your talking, if you say one word which betrays us, you will die on the spot."

Chapter Eleven

Pastor Paul Lamba, living in the forest refugee camp, decided that his first duty was to take a census of the persons under his care. He found a blank staple-bound class notebook and asked his cousin Nguvu to serve as record keeper. Nguvu was a bit older than Lamba and of slender stature. He was a quiet unpretentious man; more important, he was trustworthy. Every morning Lamba, along with other men, occupied himself with gathering food for his family. He hunted. He fished. He and his wife, Tembo, would salvage root tubers of manioc from people's abandoned fields.

Every afternoon Lamba, Tembo, and Nguvu visited homes to take the census. They made it a point to record in the notebook answers to certain questions about each household: Who lived there? What were the children's ages? Where did persons living there find food? Was it adequate? Did they have fishhooks and lines which others could borrow? Nguvu made special note of persons who could not provide for themselves, such as widows with children or the elderly. Lamba

140

and Tembo took time to listen to the complaints of people and would try to quiet their fears by counsel and by prayer.

When the pastor found persons who were not getting adequate food, he charged specific households which had ample food with the duty of feeding them. Bonds of the extended family and the African tradition of providing hospitality for those in need gave people a sense of responsibility for one another. "Always feed the orphan," their ancestors had said. "He is the child of the Elder Spirit who created you." Thus for the moment people shared what they had and staved off hunger.

To further insure the well-being of the refugees, Paul Lamba set up a network of sentries like he had seen at Mulele's high command headquarters. Lines of sentries reached out from the camp in every direction like spokes from a hub. Pairs of men were stationed at half-mile intervals along each spoke. Four pairs of men were assigned to each observation point so that one pair was on duty around the clock, and all men serving as sentries still had time to perform their duties at home. When there was news of significance, one of the pair would carry it to the next observation point toward the hub while the second man remained on duty. By this means people in the camp were kept informed of activities within a radius of up to twenty miles, and could be warned well in advance of any encroaching military or rebel

141

forces who threatened them.

In steadily increasing numbers, people came to Lamba and Tembo for help: a new family of refugees with no relatives in the camp to assist them, a man grieving over news that his younger brother was killed by rebels, a woman who wanted him to pray over her feverish child, a man who wanted him to officiate at the burial of an elderly person. The growing burden compelled the pastor and his wife to cast themselves upon the Lord. The trauma of these months tested Lamba's faith. He was not certain that his choices had always been right. When one is suddenly confronted by an unfamiliar situation, how does he always discern the will of God? Why did not God write what He wanted in the sky or reveal it in a dream to be read clearly? While Pastor Lamba did not have all the answers, he did find the strength he needed in worship.

At dawn every weekday morning he would go sit on a log in the worship shelter and wait for others to join him. A group of faithful believers came regularly. How their fellowship encouraged him! How their prayers supported him! When he recognized the help he derived from these times of waiting before God, he decided to have a period of family worship late each afternoon. He, Tembo, their ten-year-old daughter, their seven-year-old son, and a few believers would close themselves inside his windowless house, cluster themselves closely on mats on the dirt floor, and offer their singing and prayers to

God. An hour or two would quickly slip by as they lost themselves in worship. Unfailingly, a Presence would strengthen, comfort, and refresh them.

One morning when Lamba and the believers were dispersing after their worship service, the village chief approached and greeted him. "Why is it that you persist in this business of worshiping the God of the mission when everybody else has abandoned it?" he asked.

Lamba was confounded. "First go sit down at my house," he replied. He wanted to postpone a confrontation until people were at a distance. Shortly he followed the chief to his house and sat down with him.

"Father," the pastor said respectfully, "do you think that the God of the mission differs from the God of our ancestors? There is only one God, the Creator of all things. Our forefathers worshiped Him. We Christians worship Him. Why do you ridicule us? When was it that our forefathers sought surpassingly the intervention of their departed ancestral spirits? Was it not in times of war and distress? Is this not a time of distress? If God does not help us in such a time, who will?"

"True, we are in a time of great trouble," the chief conceded. "But people of the revolution say that worshiping God in the manner that missionaries taught us no longer has value. Now that the missionaries are gone once and for all, we are not to keep on imitating them."

"I am not teaching people to imitate our missionaries," Lamba explained. "I am leading believers in their worship of the God of life. When people turn their hearts around and begin to follow the Son of God, how do they act? They begin to sit quietly at peace. They tend to their own affairs. They show love to their neighbor. Think for yourself. As we sit here in the jungle as refugees, who are those perpetually causing trouble? You and your elders are trying to settle their disputes all the time. Are they persons who have the custom of listening to my teaching and worshiping God? If this custom helps make people good, why do you say it no longer has value?"

"It's no affair," the chief apologized.

"My chief, I don't want people to twist up your understanding of this matter," Lamba sought to counter the instruction of those who apparently were influencing the chief against him. "I accepted to carry this burden only after you and the village elders promised to work together with me like the fingers of one hand. The suckling infant knows that its life is in the breast. The village wise man knows that his life is in the cooking pot. Christians persist in their custom of worshiping because they know that their life comes from Christ. The ancestors said, 'Don't ridicule the woman who cooks your food.' I am carrying out the work you gave me to do. If you want to help me as you promised, then put an end to the foolishness which is in some people's heads that it is wrong to worship God any longer."

"I have heard your words," the chief replied emphatically. "I will not trouble you with the matter again."

Silently, unremittingly, the weeks slipped into months. Apparently people spread the word of the jungle camp. Newcomers seeking haven arrived almost daily. It was unthinkable to turn them away. Soon people could not find adequate food. They stripped fields near the camp and began searching for food in more distant areas. Sentries at their scattered posts of duty reported the location of possible food sources. Refugees followed these leads and penetrated rebel-threatened districts in hopes of foraging manioc from abandoned fields. Slowly, relentlessly, all able-bodied persons were drawn into a desperate dawn-to-dark struggle to keep hunger at bay.

It was during this time that one day a newcomer brought Pastor Lamba a note. The folded paper was soiled and dog-eared from the many hands through which it had passed. Lamba deciphered his almost illegible name penciled on one side of it. He recognized the handwriting. It was that of Pastor James Ilunga. He unfolded the paper — a lined sheet torn from some student's notebook — and read:

Pastor Paul Lamba,
Greetings to you and to your family. Are you still where you were when I came to see

you? The revolution is causing much hardship everywhere. However, its leaders are certain they will eventually triumph. When I see how they have dedicated themselves to their cause, I believe that what they say is true. Now is the time when leaders of the revolution must be rebuked and admonished from the Word of God. This is my work. I beg of you to come help me. What we teach them now will help much with how they view the church when they begin to rule our land. To the present, I believe that you are in great danger if you stay where you are. If you and your family come and join me, I promise that you will be protected from anyone who someday might want to take reprisals against you. Let us pray for one another.

Your brother in Christ,
Pastor James Ilunga

Paul Lamba recalled Pastor Ilunga's visit. It had been just prior to the unexpected appearance of the two military scouts, after which the village people had decided to vacate their homes and move to the forest camp. The young pastor had been so enthusiastic then, so certain that his choice was right: he and his family had plenty of meat for food, they were well protected, he was working to influence leaders within the movement, the only persons to fear were government soldiers.

But Lamba read between the lines of the note

that Ilunga's situation had now changed. Enthusiasm had waned. Everybody was enduring hardship. What were the kinds of hardship Ilunga and his family were enduring? There was even a slight hint of Ilunga's uncertainty about the ultimate outcome of the revolution. That evening when Lamba was sitting alone with Tembo at an outside fire, he gave her the letter. She bent low into the firelight, read it, disconcertingly readjusted her body on the stool, and sat gazing into the fire.

"I showed it to you only that you know about it," Lamba said reassuringly. "God wants us to stay where we are. Look at this great crowd of people He has given us to shepherd! It is true that we are in trouble here. I don't know how our troubles will end. But I would never go with you and the children to join Ilunga. I fear a net is surrounding him and his family without their knowing it. Ilunga and other pastors we have worked with — will we ever see them again?"

He was lost in his thoughts for a few moments, and then suddenly added, "Do you think we need to keep that letter? Why don't you throw it in the fire?"

She stretched out her arm and dropped the paper onto the glowing bed of coals, obviously relieved to learn that their feelings were identical and that the matter was closed.

Lamba knew well their own problems. For the greater part of each succeeding day he struggled to cope with them. He had left Nguvu in

147

charge of the census. One day he asked to see the record book. He discovered that the number of persons in the camp now approached one thousand! Why had Nguvu not kept him informed of how the camp was growing? Sometimes he wished that his cousin were more assertive. Each new arrival of refugees made the search for food more desperate. It was impossible to any longer keep tab on the welfare of everybody. Lamba and Tembo continued their worship services, joined the frantic search for food, and during what time was left, visited as many homes as they could. Then one day something happened which showed the pastor that the crisis was out of control.

It was late one afternoon when Lamba and his wife were called to the hut of a family from his home village. An infant daughter had died. They found the mother seated on a mat on the ground, stripped to the waist in mourning. The dead infant lay naked across her legs. Its limbs were like broomsticks and its tummy was bloated. The mother's body was pathetically thin and her breasts hung flat and empty. There could be no question about it, the baby had died of malnutrition. Lamba and Tembo stayed at the home until late that night to offer comfort. When they returned to their own house they found their children sleeping. They laid down onto their mats for the night and for a while stirred wakefully. Finally Lamba mustered courage to articulate his fears.

"Tembo, do you know what killed that child?"

"Hunger."

"The father of that child — why did he not come tell us of such great suffering?"

"Because he sees others around him also suffering from hunger. Pastor, are we still telling ourselves that everyone is finding enough to eat? That is a fable. There is no way of knowing the trouble concealed under all these hut roofs. If everybody in this village who sits with hunger came to tell us, where would we find food for them? Could we feed the birds of a forest?"

Lamba feared that she was right. His mind conjured a specter of what could lay before them. He shuddered in the darkness.

"Mother," he said tremulously, "the thought of children suffering and dying from hunger makes my body weak as water."

He pondered their crisis for a while, sighed deeply, and began to pray aloud:

"My God — the God of all power — You gave me the work of shepherding this flock of sheep. At first I cared for them well. But how can I care for them now? Their numbers exceed my strength. They are worried, I cannot comfort them. They are hungry, I cannot feed them. They watch their children die, I cannot help them. How can I lighten their suffering? You created all these people. Your Book says that You do not want righteous people to suffer. You do not want their children begging bread. It says that You are a Father of love who knows everything

149

we need and who hears our cries. I have no one else to look to. Hear my cries for these people. Comfort us with Your Holy Spirit. Bare Your arm of strength and bring an end to this time of trouble because You Yourself see that, except these days be shortened, one by one, we will perish."

Chapter Twelve

Sixty guerrillas armed with guns escorted Stephen Kimeya toward the opposite end of the camp to a hutch. In it Kimeya saw a low table on which sat a battery-powered transceiver identical to those used on the mission stations. He suspected that the transceiver had been confiscated from Mudidi. He noticed that the transceiver switch was already in its "on" position. He sat down at the table. His guards packed around him like crows surrounding a cadaver. He knew Mulele was listening. He breathed deeply, picked up the microphone, and pressed its button to transmit.

"9TX63. I am calling 9TX63." He waited, praying his missionary friend would answer. He called again, and a third time, waiting.

"This is 9TX63," the voice of his white friend was strong and clear. "Who are you?"

"This is Stephen Kimeya."

"Stephen Kimeya! Is that really you? Or is someone impersonating you? We heard that you were dead. Where are you?"

The prisoner hesitated.

"I'm in the hands of soldiers," he replied. It was a half-truth designed to satisfy those watching him. "How are things there?"

"Everything is going well here. The big matter is that of teachers' salaries. I have four months of salary money to give you. It is urgent that the teachers be paid, or they will stop working. Do you have a way to come here and get it?"

Stephen was dumbfounded. Before he had even raised the issue the missionary had proven in the hearing of them all that teachers' charges against him of embezzlement were false. His purpose for broadcasting was achieved.

"I am not able to come," he replied. "It is necessary that you yourself go with the money to Mudidi and pay them."

"There is much fighting between here and Mudidi; no one can get through. But inasmuch as you are in the hands of soldiers, explain the situation to them. The government does not want the schools to close. Soldiers will escort you there."

"There is no way for me to come," Kimeya repeated.

"Then arrange with your local government man to come with soldiers and meet us halfway along the main road at the river," his friend rejoined. "You set the time and we will meet you there."

Kimeya struggled to conceal his anguish.

"My situation is very difficult. I cannot come."

The missionary paused, suggesting his suspicion.

"Whose transmitter are you using?" he asked.

"It belongs to the soldiers."

"I'm not reading you well on this frequency. Change to channel number two."

Kimeya suspected the request was calculated to disclose what kind of transmitter set he was using. The guards watched unsuspectingly. He changed channels and thereby confirmed that he was using a familiar mission transceiver.

"One other matter," the missionary added. "You have been chosen to go to Belgium for study. Your scholarship money is waiting for you. We want to arrange your travel plans. How soon will the soldiers bring you out?"

The missionary's questions, shot at him like a hunter's arrows, were coming perilously close. His emotions buffeted him mercilessly. He feared losing self-control.

"Give the scholarship to someone else. I stand between life and death."

He released the microphone button, dropped his head onto his arm, and sobbed uncontrollably. For a few moments he was oblivious to his surroundings. Then he felt someone jarring his shoulder.

"Let's go." It was a guard. "Mulele is calling you."

Stephen felt weakness like that of a year's illness. He struggled to his feet and went with them. They found the rebel commander at his house still seated by the radio.

"Today I accept that your words are true,"

Mulele exclaimed. "You did not raise the matter of teachers' salaries, the missionary himself did. You are vindicated."

"I am glad you are convinced that I did not embezzle their money. On the basis of what you have just heard, you yourself can decide whether or not their other accusations against me are true."

"I have already decided. Those teachers are troublemakers." Mulele scowled. He was gesturing angrily. "Their accusations are false. I want to call them here and tell them so. I'll have them executed. If I don't, they'll keep on causing other innocent people to suffer as they have you."

"No. Don't have them killed. The schoolchildren need them. Let them do their work of teaching. In due time they will come to understand the foolishness of what they have done."

"I will decide that matter later," the commander said. "As for you, from this moment you are freed from your prison. You speak truth like the voice-piece of God. You will work for me. You may go anywhere in the camp you choose. But for the present it is dangerous for you to go outside."

The broadcast incident gave Kimeya new status among camp personnel in general. Once he had been dubbed "that friend of the Americans." Now they called him "that speaker of God." But the incident also convinced them that his release could endanger their security. This probably explained why Mulele detained him.

"If he ever reaches our enemies," rebels told each other, "he'll tell them the truth about us just as he told the truth here. Then we'll no longer be able to hide."

Freed from prison, Kimeya could share the "privileges" of camp life. Officers parceled out loot brought from rebel raids and partisans reveled in the temporary creature comforts it afforded them. But Kimeya was also required to carry his share of camp duties. One day he was taken into the open-sided shed near Mulele to a table and typewriter and was put to work as one of the rebel commander's secretaries. He typed warrants to be served on accused persons. He made carbon copies of excerpts from a book of communist ideology to be distributed to political chiefs in other training camps. He typed official minutes of daily court proceedings.

Although grateful to be released from prison, he found camp life increasingly vexing. His body could not adjust to the austere diet. More and more, he found the nature of his duties repulsive. Judgments against offenders were heartless and vindictive. He frequently protested those made against Christians. Eventually he found the atmosphere of cruelty suffocating. Amazingly, it did not destroy his own sense of compassion.

One afternoon during free time when Kimeya was walking just outside the camp perimeter, he was startled to discover Maurice Gimbo, a fellow clansman from Mudidi, digging a hole with a spade. Gimbo had been a prosperous businessman and frequently had given generously for causes of the church. His tear-streaked face reflected despair.

"Keeeeeya . . . Gimbo! What are you doing here?"

"I'm digging this hole for them to bury me in at eight o'clock tomorrow morning."

"For what crime?"

"Because of the riches I had. When they came to confiscate merchandise from my store, I protested. So they have condemned me as an obstructor of their revolution."

The rebels had cut off the man's pants legs. Stephen looked on unbelievingly.

"Did they try you?" he asked.

"No. When they told Mulele about me he became terribly angry and condemned me to die." He looked at Kimeya pleadingly. "Brother, if we are not of the same tribe — if we are not of the same village — if we are not of the same clan — if I do not have the reputation of being a helper of people — then allow them to treat me as they wish."

Kimeya went to Mulele's right-hand man, Kavungu.

"I want to talk to Mulele."

"What do you want to see him about?"

"About the case of Gimbo."

"You always want to stir up trouble between us and people from the mission. Whenever we sentence one of them you protest. Go to Mulele yourself, see if he accepts to release the man."

156

Mulele was in the sitting room of his house seated at a table. Stephen entered unannounced and stood before him.

"I know what you've come for," the commander declared. "I won't hear your words. Get out."

Kimeya stood motionless.

Mulele nodded to a guard standing inside the doorway. "Take him out of here."

"If you want to renounce your own claim of being one who hears the complaints of people, then you'll have me taken out of here," Kimeya rejoined. "But if one day you are caught in distress and need to complain, who will show you mercy?"

"That man is counselling you as if he were your grandfather," the guard remarked. "Why should I not throw him out?"

Mulele sighed acquiescently.

"Gimbo keeps complaining about the loss of his wealth," he said. "Under our government there is no such thing as one person having wealth. It's good to kill him so he stops talking about it."

"When I first arrived here you explained to me that you do not sentence a person unjustly," Kimeya replied. "You first scold him two or three times before you punish him. You didn't scold Gimbo a second time. You didn't even scold him a first time. Straightway, you condemned him. Today he is digging his grave. Are you following the words you told me that day?"

The commander's body muscles tensed. His face blackened with anger. He hesitated indecisively, then sent a messenger to call the supervisor of prisoners. When the supervisor arrived Mulele announced his decision: "Gimbo, the one you have digging his hole, don't bury him in it. We'll bring him to trial first."

Gimbo was tried and sentenced to two months in prison. He served his time and, inexplicably, was set free.

Weeks slipped into months. Kimeya's typing duties led him deeply into guerrilla tactics strategic to the movement's success. At first his fingers moved mechanically across the keyboard transferring the printed French text to an original and half a dozen carbon copies. Then gradually, his mind was awakened to the nature of the material he was typing:

INCENDIARY BOMB

Extract sap from a rubber tree and leave it in the sun until it hardens. Then cut it into small pieces. Drop the pieces into a bottle of gasoline. Close the bottle and leave it in the sun for three or four days, until the gasoline looks like oil. To prepare for use, uncap the bottle and stuff its neck with cotton to serve as a fuse. At the time of attack, shake the bottle, light its fuse, and throw. On impact it will explode and spread flames over your objective.

INCENDIARY FUSE

Soak a long raffia rope in gasoline for a week. On the edge of a village, tie the rope to the grass roof of hut after hut for the rope's full length. Then ignite one end of the rope. Instantaneously the rope fuse will set all hut roofs ablaze.

AUTOMATIC SPEAR WEAPON

Along the footpath by which the enemy may approach, select a long, slender tree concealed by vegetation. About chest-height on the tree, fix firmly a spear long enough to project across the path. Cut off the tree's branches so that it can move freely. Tie a strong, slender cord to the top of the tree and pull the tree away from the path, bending its top toward the ground. Pass the cord through three or four misaligned loops close to the ground; these loops reduce strain on the cord. Pass the cord across the footpath about three inches above the ground and tie it to a stake opposite the tree. Then with a sharp knife, carefully fray the cord where it crosses the path. When the foot of a passerby strikes the cord and breaks it, the tree will thrust him with the spear.

Kimeya's conscience raised its voice in protest. By helping circulate such information he was supporting the revolution. He, a person of God, was helping to inflict suffering, to destroy, to murder. With the passing of each day, his inner suffering mounted. Again and again he turned to the Bible seeking strength and guidance. What were his alternatives? He could openly defy Mulele and be tortured or executed. He could commit suicide. But then his mind would return to the Macedonian call, which made either of these alternatives seem a betrayal of his faith.

Meanwhile, those working with him informed Mulele of his linguistic skills. He was conversant in half-a-dozen languages. He was given the task of translating radio scripts used in propaganda broadcasts into area vernaculars. Then, under supervision of an armed guard, he was required to broadcast the scripts via the mission transmitter. These duties only intensified Kimeya's pangs of conscience.

At the same time Kimeya noticed signs that the revolution was losing momentum. The rebels brought an increasing number of people to Mulele accusing them of wanting to defect to the enemy. Their interrogation of accused persons became exhibitions of brutality. The rebels sent to villages on food details reported that violence was necessary to gain villagers' cooperation. Within rebel ranks, reciprocal accusations eroded morale and disintegrated common commitment to the cause of the revolution.

Epidemic suspicion, festering hatred, licentiousness, unbridled savagery, and the loathesome nature of Kimeya's work all combined to create an atmosphere he found insufferable. His Bible reading kept fresh the Macedonian call. To the call was now added the impression to return to Mudidi mission. He resisted the thought. Were these impressions pure imagination? If they had some purpose, why did not God in some way intervene and remove him from this place to make their fulfillment possible? Kimeya was pressed toward the bleak despair he had felt during the last days of his solitary confinement. Inasmuch as he had little hope of ever escaping, why should he not risk provoking some crisis in hope of changing his situation?

When urged to join a military attack he refused and made sardonic remarks about the kinds of weapons rebels were using to wage their revolution. At the close of a daily broadcast, he discarded the transceiver fuse and feigned innocence the next day when the transceiver proved inoperative. When told to drink palm wine in the presence of Mulele and some thirty assembled rebels, he refused, and dared to witness boldly of his faith in Christ. In other ways he risked making himself a nuisance. But it did not provoke the results he had expected. While other offenders less obstreperous than he were severely punished, the rebel leaders made lighthearted banter of his conduct. He began to wonder if his life was charmed. Perhaps his linguistic skills made him so valuable to his superiors that they were determined to put up with him at any cost. So Kimeya's despair deepened. While he was sick of living, neither could he die.

Then to his emotional despair was added physical illness. His legs began to swell. He did not know why. His limited diet had caused him to lose much weight, but he was no more emaciated than most others living in the camp. No one else he knew suffered from leg affliction. Neither rest nor bathing with hot packs helped. Instead, the swelling worsened until pain made it difficult for him to get up off his sleeping mat.

"If God is really still paying attention to me," Stephen pondered, "why should this happen to me on top of all my other troubles?"

Then, during a long, wakeful night, he heard what seemed a persistent voice. He knew it was the Spirit of God.

"Go back to Mudidi mission."

"No, Lord," he replied. "I'm tired of all these troubles. I have no strength to endure more of them."

"Return to the mission," the voice insisted.

Suddenly, he recalled that final service with the missionaries, and his affirmation to them: "If you commit us into the hands of God, we will pass through these troubles and survive." Everybody was crying. They had sung a hymn to pledge themselves to one another: "We will work 'til Jesus comes."

"All right, Lord," Kimeya finally conceded. "That is what I'll do if You want me to. Now

162

show me the means by which I am to do it."

Then there took form in his mind a plan whereby he might use his illness to advantage. He wondered if it might really work. It was worth a try. The next morning he asked two rebels to help support him while he walked. He went to see Mulele.

"Chief, look at my legs," he said. The skin was stretched shiny-tight to his thighs. "You know how long I have suffered with them. Now it is very difficult for me to walk. There is one place I know where people have medicine to help me. That is at the hospital at Mudidi. Why don't you have mercy on me and send me there with someone so that this suffering of mine can be finished?"

The commander-in-chief paused to deliberate.

"Perhaps your idea is good," he responded. "We need you, but you are not able to help us in such a condition. When you are healed, will you return to help us?"

"Aren't you ruler of our land? Why would I despise your authority and refuse to return?" Kimeya hoped that his flattery had disguised his insincerity.

"Very well, Speaker of God. You are a man of true words. I will prepare a letter instructing the director of the hospital to take good care of you. I will put you into the hands of two men who will accompany you."

Kimeya struggled to conceal his astonishment.

"Thank you for answering my request," he replied.

The two rebels helped Kimeya return to his sleeping mat. He had spent six months in the hideaway command headquarters of the revolution. He was more than ready to leave.

Chapter Thirteen

Sona, the wife of Stephen Kimeya, rested on a floor mat in the village hut of a Christian friend. She pondered her new crisis. It seemed to her that from the day Kimeya was taken away, life had been an unending series of crises. Kimeya's arrest and deportation had not pacified his antagonists; they refocused their harassment upon Sona. Friends had feared for her life. They took responsibility to safeguard her and her two small daughters. They persuaded her to go with her children into hiding. From that time on, the three of them had lived like hunted prey, being moved by caring relatives and Christian friends from one inconspicuous village to another, and then on to another, before the rebel pursuers could learn of their whereabouts.

Such a way of life would be demanding under ordinary circumstances. But she was pregnant. This was her sixth month. During the fourth month she had begun bleeding. She had prayed much about it and had tried to rest as much as possible. But each time when there seemed to be improvement, she and the children were forced

165

to journey on to another village. She hemorrhaged. For a while she was afraid, wondering if the flow would ever stop. The incident had forced her to a conclusion: there was little likelihood that she could stay in the village and ever get better. In fact, the probability was that her life and that of her unborn child hinged upon her getting help.

Who could come to her aid in such a plight? Her thoughts went immediately to Kapala, father of Kimeya. Her in-laws had always been understanding and supportive and Kapala had a reputation for effectively handling difficult situations. But Mudidi was some thirty-five miles away through area harassed by the jeunesse and she wasn't even certain that her in-laws were still there. Nevertheless, she felt impelled to try and send word to them. When she saw her hostess emerge from the backyard kitchen hut, she called her.

"Musula. Could you come here?"

The woman entered and sat in a wicker chair near the door. Sona informed Musula of her hemorrhage the night before and of her desire to call Kapala.

"Is there some way of sending him word?" Sona asked.

"Let's tell your problem to the Christians," Musula replied. "They will put the matter before God, then they will hunt for wisdom by which to finish it."

They circulated word of the problem to village

Christians who met and laid the matter before God in corporate prayer. Then two men volunteered to disguise themselves as rebels and to make the foot-journey to Mudidi.

Words could not describe Sona's sense of indebtedness to fellow-Christians during those days. From village to village, every cluster of believers she had encountered provided her untold solace and strength in this raging storm. Now while believers awaited the return of the messengers, their prayers seemed to affect her with a support she could physically feel. Her bleeding abated. Her heart was filled with gratitude to God.

Toward noon of the third day, Sona was resting on a mat outside her sleeping hut when the two messengers returned. Kapala was with them. He had brought a bicycle. Christians rejoiced for this sign that God was answering their prayers. While those surrounding Sona had shown her every kindness, she felt a lifting of her burden when Kapala arrived. Seeing him brought back memories of happiness and security and home and made her feel that somehow things would come out all right. After the newcomers exchanged greetings with the village people and reported highlights of their trip, Kapala and Sona were left alone.

"The two men arrived and told me of your trouble," Kapala said, "and at that very time I began the journey to come to you. How are you?"

"That night before they left to call you, I lost much blood. Because of it, my body still feels weakness. But God had mercy on me. When I remain at rest, I bleed only a little. But first tell me — have you heard any news about Kimeya?"

"When I learned that they had taken him to Mulele's camp, I sent him a package with his Bible in it. No one has returned with the package. I expect he has received it. From time to time, journeyers coming from that direction bring word that he is still alive. Church people at Mudidi never cease praying for him."

"The God who feeds the birds, will He fail to hear our cries?" Sona wondered aloud.

They sat in silence for a few moments, their thoughts dwelling on Kimeya, their loved one, and on their hope in God.

"We will not fail to keep praying for him," Kapala reassured. "But for now we need to talk about your trouble. You say that your bleeding has not stopped. Do you think you will recover if you remain here in the village?"

The woman sighed deeply.

"I am caught in the middle of two things," she said. "If I remain here without medicine to help me and I hemorrhage again, bleeding may not stop. I would die, and the child also. But it is a great distance to the hospital at Mudidi. If I try to go the jeunesse finding us in the path could torment us. The journey may cause hemorrhaging to start again. I and the child could die before we get there. If I arrived at Mudidi still

168

with life, would the enemies of Kimeya allow me to rest?"

Kapala pondered the problem. Vagabond rebels were a threat. Sona was large and heavy. Balancing her on a bicycle for thirty-five miles of dirt roads would be no simple undertaking. And one fall could prove disastrous. But he saw no alternative.

"Chief Mazemba does not hold enmity toward Kimeya as he once did," Kapala replied. "He and his people are strengthening themselves to resist the rebels. If you reach the hospital, I see no way the rebels could harass you. I carry great indebtedness. Someday I must give an account of myself to Kimeya and to your parents for what I did to help you. How will I stand before them without shame if I leave you to die here in the village? It is a great distance to Mudidi. The journey will be hard. But if it is a matter of your dying, let it happen in the path while I am trying to help you."

The decision was painful for Sona to make. It would mean saying goodbye to her children for what could be the last time. She understood the risks, but with haunting misgivings, she agreed to go.

Word spread through the village that Kapala would try to take Sona to the Mudidi hospital. Kapala found a sturdy wicker chair. He placed it onto the bicycle luggage carrier. He fastened long, sturdy sticks down its back and tied them firmly along the carrier supports to the hub. A meal was prepared. They ate. Then Christians encircled them, and kneeling in the open air, committed them to God. Sona endured the deepest pain upon leaving her children. She did not tell them that this could be a final farewell; they were too small to understand. She encouraged them to be strong and promised that they would see each other again. Strong arms helped ease her into the chair. Kapala immediately perceived that the weight was too much for him to balance safely in riding. He would simply walk alongside the bicycle, pushing it.

"Stay well," he said in farewell as he turned to leave. "Remember us before the Creator."

"Go well," bystanders responded. "May the Father above guard the both of you."

Sona could only entrust herself to God and to the man who was trying to help her. At first the tilting of the bicycle made her fearful, but gradually she came to entrust herself to Kapala and his firm grip on the handlebars. She watched the man, dressed only in short pants with a machete slipped beneath his belt, his lean leg muscles flexing prominently with each step, to keep the bicycle upright. Skillfully he guided the wheels to skirt rougher places in the road to ease her jostling. She marveled at his patience and compassion. They kept moving, tediously, steadily forward. They traveled without incident the rest of that day and stopped at a village for the night. Sona noticed her bleeding; it had not abated, but neither had it worsened. She did not feel unduly exhausted. Her heart was encouraged. God had been good to them that day. If her body could withstand the strain of another full day, on the third morning they should arrive at Mudidi.

The following morning they were journeying across a long expanse of treeless prairie when suddenly Sona felt an abdominal pain which at first startled her. Fear gripped her. She would not believe it. After a short time the pain recurred. Could it possibly be? She grimaced until the pain eased, and said nothing to Kapala. She began praying, "Oh, my God — on top of all our other troubles why does this happen?" The pains recurred regularly with increasing intensity. Her situation was desperate. There was no possible way to continue.

"Father," she announced to Kapala, "I am caught in the pains of childbirth."

He stopped, paused only for a moment, and began acting with a resoluteness which suggested that he had already weighed such a possibility. He helped ease her off the bicycle and sat her in the road. Then he slipped the machete from his belt and began chopping at the tough grass roots along the roadside to make a smooth place for her to lie down. The traditional dress of women includes a loose cloth wrapped around the waist which hangs over the skirt. Its purpose is utilitarian: to tie an infant onto the mother's back, or to bind loose articles into a bundle for carrying on the head. Sona spread her waist cloth onto the freshly cleaned ground and lay down. The sky was overcast, subduing the heat of the sun.

Sona had never suffered long labor with the births of her children. Pains were sharp and frequent now. Kapala, his face reflecting steadfast faith, turned and left. She did not blame him for leaving. She knew he was not abandoning her. How could she expect her father-in-law to perform the duties of a midwife? Between pains she contemplated the coming ordeal of delivering herself. Was there no one to help? She knew her body was weak from loss of blood. She felt so desperately alone. Her thinking began to fog into a swoon.

Kapala hoped he had concealed his feelings of desperation. He had told Sona that if she had to die, he preferred it be in the road on their way to Mudidi than in a faraway village. Was it really going to end this way?

"Father of love," he prayed. "I am finished. There is not one more thing I can do. If You see that it is good for one of Your children who loves and trusts You to die for no reason alone out here on the prairie, that is Your business."

Something white at a distance caught his eye. It was a large porcelain-enamel basin moving slowly along just above the height of the grass. Looking closely he discerned the heads and shoulders of two women returning along a footpath from the stream.

"Mothers with me," he shouted. "Come help me!"

They stopped and looked his direction. They probably suspected he was a rebel plotting some stratagem.

"Mothers," he called again. "A woman here is caught in labor pains. Come help her."

They hesitated and then began to cautiously approach him. Kapala breathed a prayer of thanksgiving and begged God to continue drawing them toward him. As they slowly approached he called to reassure them.

"Stop fearing. My daughter-in-law has been bleeding for days. I was trying to get her to the hospital at Mudidi. Now labor pains have caught her. Won't you help her?"

They arrived close enough to see the form of a woman lying along the road, then they rushed to her side. One helped the other set her basin of fresh, clean water onto the ground. They were older women, wise in the ways of village life. They removed their waist cloths and set to work. Kapala shook his head in wonder. "You are angels sent from God," he said. "I'll be waiting close by."

One of the women nodded. He walked a few yards up the road to wait. He praised God for showing them His mercy and then continued to intercede for Sona. After some time one of the women approached him.

"Do you have a knife to cut the cord?" she asked.

"Only this." He drew the long machete from his belt and offered it. "How are things?"

"She gave birth to a girl-child. It was dead. She is not finished yet." The woman took the machete and left.

Was Sona to bear twins? Kapala could only wait and pray. At length the woman returned.

"It is finished now," she said. "She gave birth to a second girl-child, it is still living. The mother is weak, but if we take good care of her, she should recover. Here is the machete. Dig a hole to bury the dead child and the afterbirth. My relative will stay with the mother and her baby. I'm going to the village to call some people to come help us."

Kapala completed his duties, then returned to squat by Sona's side to comfort her. Soon the woman returned with three men who carried a heavy blanket and a sturdy pole. They spread the blanket onto the ground beside Sona, carefully shifted her to its center, then tied its opposite ends securely to the pole. Then two men hoisted the ends of the pole onto their shoulders and carried Sona hammock-fashion toward the village. The woman had brought a wicker basket cushioned with clean cloths. She laid the new-born baby onto the cloths, carefully covered the basket with her waistcloth to provide shade, lifted the burden onto her head, and followed the men. Kapala watched the proceedings, marveling. Then he picked up his bicycle with the now-empty chair and pushed it along at the end of the line.

Before nightfall the second infant died. Sona

was too weak to mourn. She learned that these two women, total strangers, had shown her such kindness because they were Christians. They had known her mother when they were children. For weeks Sona seemed to linger between life and death. Cut off from her husband and children, she began to sink into mental despair. Kapala, in a desperate effort to keep hope alive, rode his bicycle through war-threatened areas to a distant village and returned with Sona's mother. As the drip-drip-drip of water overcomes the hardness of stone, Kapala believed that persevering effort could surely overcome the hardest problem.

With the arrival of her mother, Sona's spirits lifted and she began a long, slow recovery. When she had gained sufficient strength, Kapala and others took her the rest of the way to Mudidi, where she was admitted to the hospital. Friends brought her children to rejoin her. Upon her release, she and her children went to live at their house. The rebels had ransacked it, but it was still their home. She continued taking medicine as an outpatient. Her ordeal with childbirth was ended. As she reminisced on the events of those dark days, she was overwhelmed with admiration for Kapala. He had cleared himself of indebtedness. He could render to Kimeya and to her parents an account that was faultless. For her, the primary ordeal now was to endure the prolonged absence of Kimeya. She began wondering if it would ever end.

Chapter Fourteen

Late one night Pastor Paul Lamba, seated alone outside his forest house, gazed into the dying embers of a fire when he was startled by the sound of a subdued cough. He looked up and in the dim orange glow made out the form of a slender bewhiskered man dressed only in a tattered loincloth.

"Greetings," the pastor announced. "Come and sit down." He motioned to a low stool opposite him.

The man hesitated and then accepted the invitation. He squatted onto the stool, the veins and muscles standing out on his gaunt limbs. He was a young man, but his sunken eyes and his deep-lined face gave him a look of age beyond his years. He sat with his arms crossed on his knees and stared into the fire.

"Were you wanting to talk with me?" Lamba asked.

The man glanced upward at the pastor and then looked back into the fire. He sighed heavily, introduced himself, and began his story.

"I have a wife. I had three small children. I was

a Christian for a long time. For thirteen years I worked in the homes of missionaries. Then came this time of trouble. We just arrived here today. Inasmuch as pastors are persons of renown, I have heard about you for a long time. Since we arrived today the voice of my heart has been telling me to come speak to you of my problems. I have been arguing with it, but now I have come. Pastor, my strength is finished. My faith has died."

Lamba watched the man compassionately, waiting for him to continue.

"When the rebels chased away the missionaries, I with my wife and children returned to my home village. The jeunesse were in authority there too. I refused to get mixed up in their affairs. Their reign caused us much suffering. Salt disappeared. Clothing wore out. When our tatters were insufficient to cover our nakedness, we returned to making loincloths like our forefathers. When people got sick there was no medicine. The rebels forbade us to worship; they forbade our children to go to school. They made a rule which said that no one was to set foot on the school and chapel yards again. Whenever they found someone reading a book or using something retained from the white man's era they judged him, found him guilty, and harassed him. In spite of all this, people resisted their authority. One day the rebels arrested a group of young men. They wanted to determine who was giving the village people hard heads. They judged us. They decided that five among us were to blame. They tied their hands and feet. Then, with everybody in the village watching, the jeunesse buried these five men alive. When we watched this, our hearts turned to water. There was not a person left with courage to speak a word."

The man paused. Reliving the ordeal had deepened the lines of stress on his face.

"Early one morning we heard the noise of machine guns," he continued. "We knew that government soldiers were coming. As is their custom, they were shooting into villages and burning the homes to destroy rebels they feared were hiding there. To escape death we fled into the forest. There my two-year-old son became sick. It was malaria. His body kept getting hotter until he began convulsing. At that very time, a group of rebels arrived demanding that we all go with them into the heavy forest far north to get away from the soldiers. I asked them how my wife and I could travel when our child was dying. They said that orders must be obeyed, we must prepare for the journey. I had met one of the rebels before who remembered me. When I was alone with him I pleaded that he allow us to stay there overnight. Finally he agreed that we could stay if I gave him our blanket. It was the only thing we had left to protect our children from the coldness of the night. We argued until finally he said we could stay if we gave him half of the blanket. I ripped it in half and gave him his piece.

We stayed that night, but we did not sleep. My child kept convulsing. His body would shake with chills. Then it would become hot as fire. He died when dawn came, my wife holding him in her arms. Pastor, when I buried my son there in the forest, my faith died. If there is a living God in heaven, why doesn't He respond to our cries? If He is a Father who loves His children, why does He watch us suffer in such a manner and do nothing? Why does He allow our little ones to die?"

The despairing man was weeping now. He rested his forehead on arms crossing his knees and struggled to choke back a sob. Pastor Lamba waited until he felt it appropriate to respond.

"My friend, I myself feel the greatness of your sorrow. Sometimes the burden seems to surpass our strength to carry. Don't feel badly that your burden makes you ask such questions. Anyone who endures this kind of suffering will ask himself questions. It would be surpassingly difficult for us if Jesus had not warned us that such times would come. He said that evil men would hate us and accuse us and beat us and deliver us to death. He said that such things must happen before He returns. He told us that His Father sees even a sparrow drop to the ground. God watches those who cause a little one to suffer. He says that one day such persons must bear their judgment."

Lamba paused. The man was quiet now, absorbing these thoughts. Then the pastor continued.

"God can answer us by performing a miracle; but many times He answers us through other persons, often without our recognizing it. One time my burden was so great that my mind almost broke. I was on the point of killing myself. But people with good hearts found me and strengthened me. They helped me back into the path of faith again. Explain to me. Why did the rebels not find you guilty and bury you alive?"

"As God wanted it," the man shrugged.

"Tell me also," Lamba asked. "How did you and your family arrive here?"

"On the evening of the day our son died, two teachers from my home village found us. They were with their wives and children. They also were fleeing from the rebels. We came here together, six adults and nine children."

"Do you think that they found you accidentally?" the pastor asked. "God sent them to help you. True, you lost your son. God grieves with you over that. Because of evil men, His own Son died. But God has also shown you signs of His goodness. Because of the troubles in our land more people are being buried every day. You are not among them. I see you sitting here before me. You are alive. You have your wife and two children. You are here among believers who care for you and can help you bear your burden. Can you not thank God for this?"

A glimmer of understanding began to soften the lines of the man's tension-drawn face.

"Yes," he replied, his head nodding slowly.

"God has shown me mercy."

"At dawn every morning the believers meet here in this worship shelter." Lamba gestured to his right into the darkness. "The strength we have these days comes from our praying together. You should come meet with us in the morning."

"Pastor, I thank you for your words. They have strengthened me. My burden has lightened. We need your prayers. But I doubt if I will be here in the morning. We fear the rebels may be pursuing us. We plan to leave at the first cockcrowing. We want to arrive as soon as possible at another place where we believe we can surrender ourselves to government soldiers."

"Do what you think is right. The Christians here will remember you before God."

Paul Lamba prayed with the man and bade him good night. Mentally the pastor added this incident to a growing list of events in recent weeks which showed the frightening toll the revolution was exacting from those held in its grip. Even among the thousand refugees living here in the forest camp, the struggle for survival was straining the bonds of community. Everybody lived with hunger now. The protein-deficiency disease of kwashiorkor had begun to take its toll; its victims, children with broomstick limbs, swollen feet, bloated tummies, and rust-colored hair, were an increasingly common sight. The young and the aged were dying in mounting numbers. Lamba had counseled the man affirmingly. The pastor had not revealed how strongly he identified with the young father's distress. To view helplessly the prolonged suffering of innocent children brought an anguish all its own. Lamba felt like the prophet Habakkuk who complained long ago, "O Lord, how long must I call for help before you listen, before you save us from violence? . . . How can you stand to look on such wrongdoing? . . . Destruction and violence are all around me . . . and justice is never done." (Habakkuk 1:2-4).

Notwithstanding Paul Lamba still recognized advantages in their present situation. He thought of the believers whom he knew would love one another even unto death. He recalled that the rebels had made only infrequent incursions into the camp. They had caused no trouble. Perhaps it was because they knew Mulele had authorized Pastor Lamba to be in charge of people taking refuge there. Perhaps it was because the people had nothing the rebels needed.

It was now apparent that suffering in outlying areas where the rebels exercised unchallenged control was far greater. Some stories were brought by the steady trickle of arriving refugees, others were heard by sentries serving at their distant posts of duty. In those areas the toll of famine was alarming. Word came that refugees who had been hiding in the forest for over a year had begun to defect to the government military forces. Some wore waist bands of leaves or tattered gunnysacks, the trauma of their pro-longed ordeal had left them incoherent. In addition to enduring famine, people in outlying regions were now bearing the full brunt of unrestrained rebel savagery. Some of the leaders of the revolution were resorting to pure terrorism in a desperate effort to bolster flagging support for their cause. Lamba wondered how Pastor Ilunga and his family were weathering the storm.

Paul Lamba realized that he was powerless to help people in outlying regions. But what about the people under his charge? He could not escape the fact that if present circumstances were allowed to run their course, hunger-suffering in the camp would increase until it became as great as that endured by people in areas outside of it.

Was it morally right for him to allow circumstances to run their course? Was there nothing he could do to change things? Gradually he found his mind struggling to form a plan. The consequences of its failure were so frightening that he did not share his thoughts with Tembo. Was there some way of surrendering to government forces? Could he go alone — or with his family — or with his clan? None of these plans was practical, the rebels were known to take savage reprisal upon people who remained behind. Only one strategy would work, one whereby all the refugees in the camp could simultaneously be brought under the custody of government forces. How could such a plan ever be realized without the rebel forces learning of it, or without some people losing their lives? It seemed beyond the realm of possibility until a sentry coming off duty told him a story. "Do you remember Pastor Thomas Sangu who used to oversee groups of believers in villages of the region south of Kende?" the man asked.

"Yes. I know him."

"He and his wife have surrendered themselves to government soldiers."

"Have you heard how it happened?"

"We hear that when government soldiers were attacking the pastor's village, the rebels killed their officer. In retaliation the soldiers killed four village men and caught Sangu. They tied him and began interrogating him. He said he was a pastor and that the only weapon he had was his Bible. They didn't want to believe him. They slapped him and beat him relentlessly to make him tell the truth. He never changed his words. Finally he told them that his wife was ill in the forest. He pleaded with them to go with him to get her, she would verify that his story was true. They consented. He led them into the forest to a refugee camp which was abandoned. He went to a place where dry palm fronds covered the ground. Under the fronds was a stick. He knocked on it three times. His wife answered. Soldiers pushed the fronds to one side and un-covered the hole where the sick woman was hiding. They pulled her out and began asking questions about her husband.

" 'He doesn't have any gun,' she told them."

"The soldiers said, 'He told us he had a gun in the forest where his wife was hiding.'"

"She answered them, 'Then he must have been lying. He has done no one evil. The Mulelists beat him up when he refused to take a gun and go help them fight.'"

"The government soldiers finally accepted that the pastor's words were true. They took him and his wife to their lieutenant. The lieutenant told him, 'If your only weapon is the Bible, then you will help us draw people from the forest.' So Thomas Sangu has been going with soldiers to the edge of the forest and calling for people to come out. Last week seven villages of people hiding in the forest answered his call. His work has brought an end to the suffering of those people and has restored peace to the land where they lived."

Pastor Lamba was surprised that the sentry shared with him a story which intimated that surrendering to the military forces would be a way of bringing an end to their suffering. As the days drug slowly by he picked up clues that others in the camp shared the man's feelings. Lamba pondered and prayed. How could he help the people do what it seemed a growing number of them were now ready to do?

The pastor began wondering if reoccupying their home village might not be a first step toward making their desires known to military authorities. Sentries confirmed that the houses there were still intact. He dared not give insurrectionists reason to suspect that he was probing for a way to help a thousand people defect from the rebel authority to government forces. Notwithstanding, a request to abandon the forest camp and return to the village site should not give undue cause for suspicion if he could offer the area rebel commander a good reason for it. The village was along a main road by which military forces penetrating into the area must come. If people had reoccupied their homes, Lamba would be in a better position to secretly inform the approaching soldiers of his intentions and to allay the fears of the people about waiting to receive them.

One morning during the daily worship service Pastor Lamba recommitted himself to God. Today he was going to the area rebel headquarters to talk with the commanding officer. After the service he went into the house and prepared to leave. He had a short-sleeved white shirt which was fairly intact; only across its shoulders had the cloth of threadbare areas begun to separate. He was wearing his last remaining pair of trousers. Their shredded legs had been cut off long ago; now their seat was an erstwhile assortment of layered shabby patches, and their front was a gauze of tenuous fibers stretching from seam to seam. It occurred to him that they were no longer decorous for a pastor to wear. He discarded them, donned a traditional palm-fiber loincloth, girdled it with his worn leather belt, put on the shirt, and left.

He walked for the better part of an hour and reached the rebel headquarters — a cluster of huts remotely located on the forest edge. He met a pair of armed sentries, introduced himself, and asked to see the regional president. They conducted him to a hut in the center of the camp and led him inside. There behind the table sat a burly young man with a round bushy-whiskered face. A prominent scar traced its way vertically up the center of the man's forehead and disappeared into his hair. A shabby military jacket with a scattering of brass buttons hung open at his chest and exposed a strip of prodigious black hair from his throat to his waist. Lamba greeted him. The man responded curtly.

"I am Paul Lamba," the pastor began. "I supervise a camp of refugees living in the forest."

"I know you," the man seemed to warm a bit. "I've heard that you are taking good care of them. Because your people have caused no trouble, we have had no reason to come and visit you. Sit down." He motioned toward a wicker chair shiny and warped into a precarious tilting position from long use. Lamba shifted the chair against a side wall for support and sat down. The two sentries left.

"Neither have I had reason to bother you," Lamba reciprocated, "and now I don't want to take much of your time. But I see that the burden of caring for the people is surpassing my strength. Their numbers have grown. Because they live in the forest, they are no longer able to find the things that they need to stay alive. Their suffering causes me much anguish. For that reason I have come to you for help."

"What is it you want?"

"At the beginning of the revolution at places where there was fighting, the leaders encouraged village people to go hide in the forest. They assured us that we would not have to stay there for long; after a few weeks they would control things and we would be able to return to our homes. We did not refuse. We obeyed them. Now more than a year has passed since the revolution began. Food in the forest is depleted. Hunger is weakening bodies. Different diseases have begun to kill our old people and children. Everybody is beginning to ask if the revolution will keep them in their forest-prison forever. They want to return to their homes in the village. Unless they begin cultivating their fields again, they are certain that hunger and disease will overpower them."

The regional president fingered a few papers on the table and licked his lips in anticipation of replying.

"The revolution is succeeding," he said. "We will triumph, there is no doubt about it. But we are not progressing as quickly as we had planned. We are not happy to see village people suffer. Everybody is enduring hardship. But the day is coming when suffering will end. Then all of us will rejoice."

"I have not come to question you about the

revolution," Lamba replied. "I have come to ask you only one thing. I beg of you, in order to reduce the suffering of people, allow them to return to live in their village."

The man scratched his whiskers while pondering the request.

"The time is not yet sufficient for people to live openly in their villages."

"But sir, if the revolution is succeeding as you say, for what reason must people you rule continue to hide in the forest?"

The rebel leader fixed his gaze on Lamba and began drumming his fingers restlessly on the table.

"I have been appointed to rule this region. Its people are my charge. Why must I give you a reason for my directives? Are you disputing them? Are you saying that they are not trustworthy? I have told you that it is not yet time for people to live openly in their villages."

The pastor did not press the point further. He paused to recover the man's respect.

"Then please, sir. What words shall I take back to those who are looking to me for help?"

"Tell them to sit quietly. Tell them to strengthen their hearts. We know all about their suffering. When the time is right for them to return to their villages, we will send them word."

Pastor Paul Lamba politely thanked the man and left. Lamba's heart was heavy. The regional president was adamant in his refusal. Was he really convinced that the revolution would still succeed? Did he have reasons for his optimism of which Lamba was unaware? Lamba had information from camp sentries and from transient refugees which seemed to confirm that the revolution was failing. Could he be misled by such information? What was the true situation?

If there was uncertainty about the fortunes of the revolution, there was no uncertainty about the suffering it was inflicting upon people caught in it. A few days after Lamba's visit to the rebel headquarters, he heard news that disease and famine had taken the lives of all six of Pastor James Ilunga's children. The news hit him like a staggering blow in the middle of his stomach and left him with a feeling of weakness for days. The evening after word arrived, Christians gathered in the worship shelter and sang hymns and prayed until what must have been past midnight to uphold Pastor Ilunga and his wife in their ordeal. They could deeply empathize with the couple for within their own camp deaths of children were increasingly frequent.

It was not long before news came which Lamba read as an unmistakable clue to the fate of the revolution. Sentries in all directions brought the same report, thereby confirming its truth. The rebel leaders had issued a new directive: inasmuch as many lives had been lost in the course of the revolution, partisans were encouraged to have sexual relations with village females as frequently as they desired, so as to replenish the earth.

Ordinary refugees were shocked. Sexual licentiousness violated their ancestral traditions. How could rebel forces any longer profess to be allied with tribal ancestral spirits? Christians were incensed. Parents of adolescent girls were apprehensive. To date the rebels had largely ignored the camp, perhaps because its people had nothing the rebels wanted. Now they might come to claim the unmarried women. Pastor Lamba saw the directive as a desperate ploy by the insurrection's leaders to reduce widespread disenchantment among the rebel forces and to recover their support. It was a sure sign of a failing cause. It also indicated that the regional president had lied to him.

This development gave Lamba confidence that if he could find a way to lead the total camp population to surrender to government military forces, he would have aligned his people with the winning side. How could such a mass defection be planned and executed without someone leaking news of it to the rebels? One thing was certain: the village chief would have to be in on it.

Meanwhile Lamba and Tembo watched as crushing deprivation slowly and inexorably produced a daily lengthening litany of suffering. The sight was common now — people dressed in tatters, the protruding bones of their chest cavities graphically exposed. Lamba himself had lost much weight. Skin across his abdomen had begun to hang in loose sagging folds. It became increasingly apparent to him that the time was approaching when he must act. One afternoon when he and his family were sitting on the ground inside his home in worship, he noticed that his two children were not participating. They sat listlessly, gazing at the floor or wall. At first he thought of reprimanding them; then he decided to wait and discuss the matter with Tembo.

"Did you notice how the children were not worshiping with us this afternoon?" he asked Tembo when they sat alone at the fire that evening.

"Is today the first time you noticed it?" she responded somberly.

It was the first time he had noticed it. He had been too occupied with the concerns of others to recognize what was happening in his home.

"What do you mean?" Lamba queried.

"They have been acting that way for several days."

"What is the matter with them?"

Tembo looked at her husband uncomprehendingly.

"Did you think that hunger would cause everybody else's children to suffer, but not your own?"

The words struck him with staggering impact. Countless times he had comforted those mourning the loss of loved ones. Now the specter of death was casting its shadow on his own home. Why had he waited so long to do something? Had he in reality been calloused to the intensity of others' pain? He could not answer such questions now. He only knew that the moment to act had arrived.

"Tembo," he said gravely. "I can't reveal to you what I have in mind. If you will, put out the fire and go to bed. I'm going to see the chief."

Chapter Fifteen

Sona had dressed the children one morning and was tending to household duties when she noticed a strange man approaching along the road which passed in front of their home. His body was emaciated, his clothing was tattered, much of his face was covered with shaggy beard, and he limped. She looked at the man a second time, then a third, stared at him incredulously, and then screamed.

"Kimeya!"

She rushed off the front veranda and into his arms.

"Living God, You have shown us mercy!" Stephen exclaimed.

She clung to him. Then she relaxed her embrace and looked at him. It was not a dream. He was bewhiskered and dirty and ill, his legs were pitifully swollen. But he was alive and home again. She felt a surge of pity for him. She would bathe him and prepare him a good meal. Turning toward the house she noticed their two daughters standing in the footpath just off the front step. Abandoned by their mother and terri-

194

fied by the man who held her, they were wailing disconsolately, their contorted faces streaming tears.

"My children!" She rushed to comfort them. "Don't you know your father?"

They buried their faces in the folds of her skirt, at length risking to peek wide-eyed at the man still standing some distance away.

"Don't force them to come to me now," he said. "Take them inside the house." After she left with them he walked to the backyard and dropped himself gratefully onto a familiar creaking straight-backed chair.

Sona delightedly ministered to his needs. It was almost a week before his children began accepting him. Church people were exuberant about his return. He was astounded to find them praising God that he was afflicted with a leg ailment.

"Look at this surprising affair!" they exclaimed. "We were praying God would give our brother a sickness that would make the rebels set him free. That is what happened! We serve a God whose power breaks trees in the jungle!"

He went to the hospital and joined the long line of patients awaiting treatment. A senior medical aide led him into a consulting room and examined his legs.

"I'm sorry, but the large number of patients coming for help every day has depleted our stocks of medicine," he said. "We have no remedy for your leg sickness."

After that Stephen stayed at home. He walked as little as possible and applied hot packs to his legs in an effort to reduce swelling and pain.

At first he was disappointed that people at the hospital were unable to help him. Then he began to recognize it as a blessing in disguise. The failure of his leg condition to improve would postpone the threatening day when he might be forced to face the issue of returning to serve Mulele. If this was the cost of escaping a forced return to the hellish climate of that jungle camp, he would pay it gladly. In fact, he had growing reason to hope that if his leg ailment were prolonged sufficiently, intervening events might solve the dilemma for him.

There was a growing cleavage between the people of Mudidi and proponents of the revolution. Shortly after Kimeya's return to his people, a fresh incident caused smoldering resentment to burst into open flame. Four Mudidi church leaders received a summons to appear before Mulele. They went to answer it. Ten days passed. Then word came that on their return a band of the jeunesse had arrested them and now held them as hostages demanding a ransom payment of cash and animals. People close to the leaders' wives helped them scrape together the ransom. The women journeyed on foot to the rebel encampment, paid the ransom, and gained release of their husbands.

When the four freed hostages returned they called a meeting of the church council. About fifteen men representing leadership of the Mudidi congregation took their places on chairs placed in a semicircle in the front part of the church sanctuary. Stephen Kimeya was among them. The senior pastor, one of those freed, took his place as chairman behind a table facing the council. He called order and led in a brief prayer.

"I have asked Elder Kipoko who was with us on this journey to recount for you what happened," he announced.

The elder stood at his chair, commented briefly on their journey to the secluded high command headquarters, and then came to the purpose of their summons.

"Mulele said he called us to solicit our help. We can continue meeting to worship God every Sunday. We can speak from the Book of God. But the time has come when everyone must work together. When we stand in the pulpit he wants us to teach things which support the revolution. For example, he said, when the Israelites were in Egypt they were the rebels. Because of the injustices they suffered, they spoiled the land and overthrew its cruel leaders. Because they revolted they entered a land where they found riches and freedom. He said that Jesus was also a very good example. We should follow Him. He always helped the poor and the suffering. He defied the wicked leaders of His time. He revolted against their foolish laws which afflicted people. They accused Him of trying to overthrow the government. He died to set people free. Mulele said we must teach people that it is very important to support the revolution. He said he wants to wipe out the rumor that he is against the church. He needs the church. He wants people to continue worshiping as is their custom. He said he would send a representative to speak in our church to reveal to us plans for the revolution. He would appoint someone to attend all of our church meetings to listen to what we preach."

Stephen heard a few listeners snap their tongues in disgust. "What is his thinking about the missionaries?" someone asked.

"We asked him if he would accept for our missionaries to return," the elder replied. "He asked us if during all the years the missionaries were with us, they had not taught us to do all the things they were doing. We said yes. Then he asked why we still had further need of missionaries."

Council members took a moment to absorb this reasoning. Then one of them broke the silence.

"Did he give you any other instruction?"

"He said nothing more concerning the church," Kipoko continued. "But he had a word for us to bring back to Chief Mazemba and the people of Mudidi. He said we should all stop complaining about not having a stronger word of authority in the movement. The zone boundaries which group tribes together had been established long ago. We should submit ourselves to our Zone Commander Kavu and follow his directives. Mulele said that the revolution seeks peace. It will punish anyone who stirs up people against it."

Kimeya closely watched those listening. Several faces registered contempt. He suspected that the men's insides seethed like fermenting wine.

"Now relate to us what happened when you all were returning," one requested.

"We were in the path about one hour when all at once about twelve rebels grabbed us. They were hiding in the high grass; it appears they had been waiting for us. As is their custom, they were surpassingly angry. They said we had hard heads and were obstructing the revolution. They tied our hands and feet. They beat us with their weapons showing no mercy. They said we should be killed. Then they carried us to a hut, threw us onto the ground inside, and tied the door shut. We suffered. We received no food worth mentioning. We knew nothing of what was happening until our wives arrived with things the rebels were demanding. Then we were released and came home. No one else caused us any trouble."

There was a pause to absorb this new information.

"These things the elder is reporting, are they accurate?" a man asked.

"Yes, they are accurate," the pastor-chairman said. The other two leaders who had shared the experience nodded in affirmation. "Does any-one else have a question to pose the elder?" he inquired.

Elder Kipoko waited through a few moments of silence and then sat down.

"Now that you have heard the report of our elder, what is your thinking?" the chairman asked.

Council members sought an appropriate way to vent their feelings of resentment.

"An astounding affair," one ventured. "A band of worthless youth binding our shepherds hand and foot and beating them like dogs!"

Words came spilling forth.

"Rebellious children with wisdom the length of a little finger thus assaulting our venerable leaders, our instructors in the truth of God. Have the rascals no shame?"

"They follow the footsteps of their leader. Does Mulele have shame? He says his supporters follow the example of the Israelites. Truly? When the people of Israel revolted against Pharaoh, did they do such a shameless thing as this?"

"And he likens his jeunesse to Jesus? Our Lord Who pitied the suffering, our Lord Who died on the cross to pay the penalty of man's sinfulness? Mulele is corrupting the truth of God."

"Think of his arrogance! Our leaders who learned at the feet of missionaries, our leaders who for many years have matured in the knowl-edge of God. Mulele proposes to replace them. He tells them what they should be teaching. He decrees to them laws about how we are to act in the house of God!"

"Mulele is a trickster. Do you remember the fable of the friendly thorn vine that pleaded permission to grow alongside the manioc plant? The vine produced no good thing. It strangled the food plant. This man's teaching is barren. If people submit themselves to it, after some years it will strangle the church and erase the words of God from people's minds forever."

It was at a later secret meeting of Chief Mazemba and select village notables where Kimeya was able to measure the full-bloom dimensions of local antagonism toward the movement. Their bitterness broke forth in a torrent of words.

"Don't you recall the beginnings of this revolution business? Those starting it promised us the good things which come with independence. We would rule ourselves. But look how it is now. They drew the boundaries of this command zone without consulting us. They put Kavu, that stranger from an ignominious tribe, to rule over us. They tell us how to run our hospital. They tell us what to say in church. They send spies to see how we are obeying. Their undisciplined youth swagger along our streets insulting and threatening us. Some of our leaders have died at their hands. Now Mulele sends a decree ordering us to quietly submit to his authority or he will punish us. That independence they were talking about, where is it?"

"They said that Kazavubu's government had impoverished us. Their government would bring us wealth. The wealth they were promising — where does it come from? They confiscate it from those who have worked hard for it, and then divide it among themselves. For example, look what they did to our storekeepers. They killed one and looted his store. They wanted to kill another, but he was spared when he gave them his lifelong savings. They arrested Gimbo, deported him to Mulele for judgment, and took all his merchandise. Look at our poverty now. There is no cloth to buy. There is no kerosene. There is no salt. That wealth the revolutionaries promised — when will it arrive?"

"Don't you remember? They said that when the time was right, foreigners, the friends of Mulele, his teachers, would bring us wealth. They would bring us good roads, and hospitals, and schools, and work to do. They have not come. While the jeunesse were consuming their loot, we sat quietly taking care of our own affairs. Every day scores of people come to the hospital for treatment. Our medical assistant who worked all those years with the missionary doctor — he has cut open more than three hundred people and healed them, losing not one. The rebels have no medicines left to heal the sick. They have no doctor. So they want to take charge of our hospital. We still have a bit of cloth and we make our own garments. They have no clothes to wear; so they decree that every male can have only two pairs of trousers, and must give his others to the cause. We make our own soap, as missionaries taught us, and they get angry. When they fail nicer ways of laying hands on our wealth, they extort it from us by kidnapping our leaders and demanding payment of ransom."

"How can we correct such injustice? Remember how they berated the soldiers of Kazavubu for tormenting us? Now the rebels themselves, what are they doing? They abuse us in any manner which gives them pleasure. If we utter a word of complaint, in the tribunal we are always condemned and they are always justified."

Kimeya surmised that feelings of resentment between forces of Mulele and the people of Chief Mazemba now ran so strong and deep that reconciliation was impossible. It was true that the insurrectionist leaders were galled by the stubborn refusal of the Mudidi people to allow the revolution to alter their ordered lifestyle. The breach grew. Zone Commander Kavu sent Chief Mazemba a series of increasingly threatening notes demanding that the chief and his people demonstrate more loyalty to the cause of the revolution or face dire consequences. With growing frequency, bands of strange jeunesse of Mulele's Bambunda tribe swaggered through the streets of Mudidi villages, eyeing the residents threateningly.

For the most part the people of Mudidi resented such pressure tactics; their leaders continued to oppose rebel directives. As Mulele had promised, a personal representative arrived on the station and called a meeting to muster support for the revolution. The church was packed. At a subsequent date Kimeya and a leading elder called the people together again to countermand the emissary's instructions.

As Christmas of 1964 approached, the revolutionary leaders decreed that there would be no special celebration. Mudidi Christians were quick to respond. "We refuse to sit quietly this Christmas as though we'd never been taught about Christ," they said. "When Christmas day comes we will all be in the house of God as we have always done in the past. We will preach the same: how God manifested His love and redemption to us in Jesus Christ. If we are to be killed, let us die in the church rejoicing about the coming of Jesus upon the earth." On that day village people of the Mudidi area gave believers a strong show of support. Great numbers of them came to celebrate — some to show their loyalty to Jesus, others to show their defiance of the rebels.

A revolutionary spokesman circulated the theme that kindness had no place in the new order, even toward members of one's own family. Smoldering personal animosities were fanned into flame. Informants were rewarded for betraying opponents to the regime. Then followed secret arrests, detentions, and disappearances. In reprisal, Chief Mazemba began detaining messengers sent by Zone Commander Kavu. The crisis peaked early in 1965 when one day Chief Mazemba came into possession of a clandestine list of sixteen names of persons marked for death. The rebel commanders considered these persons to be key opponents of the revolution — they were local opinion leaders and intelligentsia including persons in charge of work at the hospital and at the church. At the head of the list was the name: "Chief Mazemba." That same day a messenger came from zone command headquarters with a summons ordering Mazemba to appear there for consultations. The chief called a small number of intimates to discuss the crisis.

"Do not go," they counseled. "Clearly Kavu is setting a trap for your arrest."

"Shall we detain the messenger as we have the others?" someone asked.

"No. When two fighting tribes arbitrate, they respect one another's messengers. Our refusal to send back their messenger would show insolence. It would give the rebels cause to launch war against us."

"We need time to decide the path we want to follow in dealing with this summons," others counseled. "Chief, why don't you send word to Kavu with the messenger that you will answer his call tomorrow?"

Chief Mazemba signed a note written by an aide and sent the messenger on his way. The group continued in lengthy deliberation. It finally decided that Chief Mazemba would invite Kavu and a delegation from the zone command headquarters to come to his home in the village of Mudidi for consultation. Following an ancient tribal tradition, the message was sent in the hands of an innocent girl of adolescent age who was considered immune to reprisal. The Mudidi village council felt certain that the rebels would reciprocate the respect accorded their own messenger.

Early the following morning, the girl left with the message in hand. By this time news of the crisis had spread through the neighborhood. Throughout the day, Chief Mazemba and the people of Mudidi anxiously awaited a reply from the nearby rebel headquarters. No word came until evening, when a group of local women who had been working in their fields came running into town. They were screaming hysterically.

"They killed her! They killed her! They cut off her head!"

People rushed to meet them.

"What do you mean?" they cried.

"They killed her . . . our girl who carried them the letter. Her head is stuck onto a stake alongside the path. Go see for yourselves."

A few people rushed down the path unbelievingly and soon returned confirming the news. Within moments the village was in an uproar. Women, holding their heads in their hands, staggered toward their homes howling their grief.

Men vented their rage by crying loudly to the ends of every village street:

"You who are men! Grab your weapons! We're going to war! Do you hear? To war!"

Chapter Sixteen

It was late afternoon in the forest refugee camp, the time when Pastor Paul Lamba regularly was inside his house for family worship. Today when a few believers had arrived to join him, he had asked them if he might meet with the members of his family alone? There were a few personal matters which needed attention. They granted his request for privacy and left.

Now the pastor sat on a low stool inside the closed hut. To his left Tembo sat on a floor mat sewing a patch onto a pair of ragged trousers. To his right Cousin Nguvu, attired in a loincloth, sat waiting. Along a far wall his two children reclined listlessly on their pallets. Lamba held his Bible propped on his knee, and on it, a paper. He furrowed his brow in concentration as he pressed a stub pencil against the paper and wrote:

To the Commanding Officer of soliders of the National Army:
    The chief of my village and I are overseeing a camp of refugees in the forest. People number about one thousand. They do not

support the revolution. They are suffering surpassingly. The chief and I have covenanted to find a way by which they might surrender themselves into your hands. Notice the map below. I will come and wait for you at the place I have indicated. I will wear a white shirt and a raffia loincloth. Can you come on June 21? If this day is not suitable, give me a different one. I will be awaiting you. In the name of God the Creator of all living things, have mercy on us.

Pastor Paul Lamba

The pastor recalled the road which passed in front of their village. Just beyond the village it curved to the right. About two hundred yards further on the right side of the road stood a straight towering nsanga tree, its trunk reached skyward a full forty feet before separating into boughs. This would be an unmistakable point for the rendezvous. He drew a sketch of the village site, the passing road, and pinpointed carefully the location of the tree. He perused the note carefully, nodded with satisfaction, and folded it into a small format.

"Look at its size," he said to Tembo in hushed tones while holding the folded paper up for her to see. "That is how big the patch pocket should be." He could not risk insurgents capturing a person with such a note in hand.

Lamba watched Tembo's fingers deftly form the stitches and smiled as he contemplated on

209

how well the plan was taking shape. Late last night he had visited the village chief. They had huddled closely inside a kitchen hut and had conversed in whispers to avoid leaking information to any would-be eavesdropper. The chief was overjoyed that Lamba was ready to pursue a course of action which might change the pattern of mounting human suffering. He was grateful that the pastor sought his collaboration. He understood perfectly the urgency of keeping the plan in the strictest confidence.

Occasionally in the past Lamba had been disconcerted by the retiring nature of his cousin Nguvu. But how the man's personality fit his present role! Who would suspect that this empty-handed ragged-dressed reticent older man carried a message of such import!

Tembo had finished her work now and was holding the shabby pants inside out at arm's length for observation. She had fastened the squarish patch to the inside of a leg where the cloth was sturdier, leaving the patch's top edge open. Lamba gave her the folded paper. She tucked it behind the patch, turned the pants right side out, and handed them to Nguvu. He took them, arose, turned toward a corner of the hut, pulled them onto his waist, and dropped off his loincloth.

"We may go outside now," the pastor murmured. "Nguvu, I have already told you where sentries have determined that soldiers are sitting. Go home and eat supper like you always do.

Say nothing about this to your wife. Later, if she becomes upset, I will console her. Tonight after people have gone to bed, put your feet into the path. You should already be at the soldiers' camp when they get up tomorrow morning. Don't bring me words from their mouths. Bring me a letter from their commanding officer. Tembo and I are praying for you. Go well."

Early next morning Lamba found Nguvu's wife at his door. She was disturbed about the absence of her husband. Lamba told her that Nguvu had been sent on an important mission. She should tell no one, her husband would return soon. The fact that Nguvu would return soon was uttered in faith rather than in certainty. But sure enough, early that evening when Lamba and his family were seated outside sharing a small supper-loaf of manioc mush, Nguvu came nonchalantly ambling across the camp toward where they were sitting. Lamba greeted him naturally and gestured toward the house. Nguvu went inside. Shortly he emerged wearing a loincloth. Without saying a word he went in the direction of home.

With great effort the pastor subdued his impatience and finished supper. Then he went inside, hastily wiped his hands on the ragged pants, found the patch, and retrieved a note. He was trembling with excitement. He opened the door a crack for light, unfolded the paper, and steadied it to read:

Rev. Lamba,

We trust that your words are true. We will come looking for you on June 21. But know that if one soldier is killed because we have answered your appeal, you will be held responsible, life for life.

Sgt. Mulamba, Company Commander

The words jolted him. Chills ran down his spine. His plan carried a price. It was that he lay his life on the line. But on second thought, military forces were not unreasonable in making such a demand. The rebels were using every form of intrigue to lure them into a trap. Why should they not exercise caution in responding to the appeal of a stranger? If this was the price of delivering a thousand people from their unbearable existence, he would pay it unhesitatingly. Late that night, after everyone was in bed, he went to the chief's house, aroused him, and shared with him the news.

Pastor Lamba debated how he could best use his time until the appointed rendezvous. Two concerns were paramount in his thinking now. One was his children whose health steadily continued to deteriorate. The other was the possibility of loss of life at that moment when this horde of people recognized the opportunity to renounce rebel control and surrender themselves to government troops.

The pastor was fairly certain that one reason for the poor health of his children was the lack of meat in their diet. During the hours of daylight he redoubled his efforts to find meat. By means of ingenious traps he tried to catch rodents. He dug into rotting palm trunks in search of fat grub worms. He stomped through coarse parching dry season grass which bordered the forest to catch grasshoppers.

There could well be bloodshed on that day when people suddenly realized that government soldiers had arrived. To reduce the risk of it, Lamba sought to condition the thinking of the people to receive the military forces peaceably. He exercised extreme caution, lest some rebel sympathizer suspect his motives and report that he was sabotaging the revolution. In his prayers at morning worship services he sought to heighten the expectancy of believers for an event which might bring an end to their tribulation. During daily discourse, when people volunteered complaints about hardships the rebel rule was imposing upon them, he sympathized with them, then he asked what they saw as a way out if hardships continued to grow. Thus many were drawn to articulate their secret desire to surrender to military troops and return under the jurisdiction of the central government.

By these means Lamba was able to influence the thinking of people. He felt increasingly certain that they were ready to surrender themselves to government troops. But two other matters were beyond his control. They caused him growing anxiety with each passing day.

213

Would the rebels learn of his plan and vent their wrath in savage reprisal? And would the soldiers liberate the camp in time for Lamba to save the lives of his children?

Chapter Seventeen

Stephen Kimeya had slept fitfully during most of the night, but now he was wide awake. He lay alone in pitch darkness in the bedroom of his home. His mind was churning with the events of recent weeks. He felt a lonesomeness that almost hurt. He was weary of the seeming endless strife. And he was afraid.

After rebels had decapitated the girl messenger, Chief Mazemba and his warriors attacked the revolutionary zone command headquarters. They burned down its buildings, scattered its defenders, and returned home satisfied.

For the five thousand people living under the jurisdiction of Chief Mazemba the victory of their chief's forces meant one thing: a rebel counterattack was certain. They set to preparing themselves for it.

Married men decided to send their families to tribal relatives living in small villages of a less-troubled area in the direction of Kende. Kimeya said goodbye to Sona and the children, and they left. Chief Mazemba sent out a general call-to-arms. When fellow tribesmen in outlying villages learned of Mazemba's open break with the Mulelists, they deserted the forces of the revolution to join him. Most able-bodied men in the Mudidi area responded to Mazemba's call. Kimeya still suffered from leg swelling and he stayed at home.

The rebel forces launched a counterattack. Mazemba's army fought for two days and repulsed it. Then the rebel leaders made alliances with tribal chiefs north and west of Mudidi and recruited more manpower. Now they were preparing to launch a mass assault on the forces of Chief Mazemba. It was rumored that Mulele had mustered 6,000 warriors and had come himself to lead the attack. He had issued a special command: "If you find Kimeya, take him alive. He has betrayed me. He stirs up people to oppose me. I myself want to deal with him." It could be rumor calculated to incite terror. It could be fact. In either case, it left Kimeya afraid.

There was little else people loyal to Chief Mazemba could do to prepare themselves. Some men were assigned sentry duty. With weapons in hand and observing a schedule of duty watches around the clock, they patrolled the area to herald any sign of encroaching rebels. Now everybody, like Kimeya, waited.

It was not that Stephen Kimeya feared death. While captive in Mulele's camp he had dared face it bravely. But there the issues were clearly defined. His death would have been a clear witness of his loyalty to Jesus Christ and of his opposition to the revolution. Had God delivered him then only to allow him to ignominiously die at the hands of Mulele now? It seemed that such a death would be a symbol of disgrace to his family and to his God.

Stephen had not articulated his inner fears. He did not want to imply to others that his personal welfare should take precedence over their own. Still, he believed there were those he could count on for help in case of crisis: members of the Christian community who were ready to lay down their lives for the sake of a brother, members of his own family, and, in particular, his father Kapala. They all knew the threats being made against him. They also knew that with his leg condition, he sat helpless as a pineapple on a stem.

Dawn was approaching when he heard a faint distant cry. It grew in crescendo as it was relayed along a chain of sentries leading toward town, and in an instant had arrived:

"Enemies are coming! Prepare yourselves!"

The town erupted in a hubbub of angry men's voices. Kimeya got up and pulled on a pair of short trousers. From the street in front of his house came sounds of pummeling feet and cries for battle. Men were running toward the line of attack. Then someone hammered on his front door.

"Kimeya!" It was the voice of Kapala his father. "Get up! We are fleeing! Come fast!"

Kimeya limped hastily to the front door and opened it. His father and an uncle met him, supported him beneath his armpits, and helped him down the veranda steps. There he saw another uncle and an older cousin holding his father's bicycle, a wicker chair firmly trussed to its luggage carrier. As they helped him mount into the chair he noticed a line of flames in the distance. The four men gripped the burdened cycle firmly, turned it away from the fires, and broke into a run, pushing it into the fading darkness.

They traveled all day in the direction of Kende, and late that night arrived at one of the villages where their families had taken refuge. Early the next morning a vanguard of Mazemba's warriors arrived. Through the hours they came, and finally Chief Mazemba himself. The rebels had attacked in overwhelming numbers. With incendiary weapons they had set everything aflame. Mazemba's forces had fought briefly and then retreated. The five thousand inhabitants of the Mudidi region were now dispossessed refugees. Families anxiously counted their members and hoped desperately that those missing would still arrive. After some days relatives of those still unaccounted for succumbed to grief and began mourning their dead.

These villages of refuge were located in a somewhat secluded area about twenty-five miles from Kende and separated from it by a river. The area was not yet under firm control of the

Mulelists. Village residents made adjustments to accommodate the newcomers. They shared their homes with some, helped build temporary shelters for others, and unstintingly shared produce from their fields.

Kimeya rejoined Sona and the children. Village people drove goats from a hut, then cleaned and renovated it. Kimeya and his family quickly made it their home. He discovered a measure of security there. Fear no longer gnawed him. He began enjoying his family again. Even his leg swelling began to subside. He had no explanation for it. Believers were certain that God had given him the ailment for a purpose. Perhaps now its purpose was accomplished and so God was taking it away.

Two weeks passed before scouts ventured back to Mudidi. They returned with crushing news.

"On the station the hospital and maternity buildings were burned," they reported. "The teacher training school was pillaged and part of it was burned. In the church, the rebels piled benches in the center of the floor and set them on fire. Their heat burned a large hole in the church roof. The dried palm branches laying on all the roofs helped them to burn. Wherever we found a corpse, we buried it. In the large village of Mazemba and in surrounding villages not a home remains, every one of them is burned to the ground. Those invaders wasted our land for no reason but to expend their vengeance."

Refugee church leaders listened to the report

and then said in retrospect, "We have suffered nothing which our missionaries did not warn us about long ago."

The people of Mudidi resigned themselves to their loss. They turned their attention to meeting their present needs for food and shelter. They were relieved to no longer endure the rebel harassment. They began to sleep well at night. But the reprieve was short. Early one morning during the third week after their arrival they heard the distant booming of heavy artillery in the direction of Kende. It was a clear sign that government forces had retaken Kende and were approaching. Scouts were sent into adjacent areas hoping to find safer haven for the refugees. They returned to report that insurgents were in firm control of villages on both sides of them. The people of Mudidi were in a corridor between the rebel forces. One end of the corridor terminated at the river not far from Kende, where government troops ruled. The other end led in the direction of Mudidi.

Chief Mazemba called his elders for consultation. Six men decided to attempt making contact with government forces in effort to surrender; if they were received peaceably, they could pave the way for the entire body of refugees to surrender themselves into custody of the government forces. The man left. Three days passed. There was no word from them. Periodic sounds of booming artillery became steadily louder. A second time the chief and his elders consulted.

After lengthy deliberation the chief called the heads of households of his tribesmen to make a pronouncement.

"We have heard no word from our men who went to surrender themselves to the government soldiers," he said. "It appears they were taken as prisoners or were killed. If this is what happened it shows that government soldiers count us their enemies because we have supported the revolution. If we surrender to them, we die. We know that the rebels count us as their enemies because we made war against the Mulelists at Mudidi. If we surrender to them, we die. If we stay where we are, either the rebels or the soldiers will find us here and we will die. There is no direction toward which we can look without seeing death. The proverb of our forefathers says, 'Storm always drives the child home.' Therefore I have vowed that if we must die, we will die in our homeland where our spirits will join those of our ancestors. We will prepare ourselves for the journey. Tomorrow morning we will set our feet in the path that returns to Mudidi."

Early the following morning women hoisted blanket-wrapped bundles onto their heads and men lifted small children to straddle their hips. Fearfully but resolutely, all the refugees from Mudidi began the fateful trek back to their homeland.

All that is except Stephen Kimeya, his wife, and their two children. Kimeya had painstakingly counted the cost. Staying would mean separation from those who had always helped him through times of crisis — longtime brothers and sisters in the church — and his parents. But he would not return to Mudidi and risk falling into the hands of Mulele. Moreover, Chief Mazemba still seemed to bear a grudge against him. He had heard that the rebels were now wantonly executing any whom they felt threatened their cause. To them a chicken was of more value than a human. Their desperation had driven them to the ultimate tactic of terrorism. Kimeya's mind was forming his own plan. It was foolhardy to make a decision of such import hastily. For three days after the Mudidi people left, he deliberated. On the evening of that third day he decided it was time to broach the subject with Sona. They went through the motions of eating supper and put the children to bed. Then they returned outside to sit on low stools at a fire.

"Sona, what is your thinking about our situation?" he asked.

She stared into the fire.

"I have no opinion about what is right or wrong to do. You are in charge of the household. Make whatever decision your heart tells you to."

He paused to grasp the implications of her response. Then he asked her a question to probe her deeper feelings.

"Would you like for us to sit here until either the rebels or the soldiers arrive?"

She did not answer. Her silence suggested that while she feared remaining in the village until government soldiers arrived, she had no other plan to offer. He did have a plan. This was not the first time that circumstances had pressed him to the point of dire extremity. On those previous occasions, when he had become convinced of the rightness of a course of action, he had pursued it with bold and reckless abandon, irrespective of consequences. What had served him well then should serve him well again. He mustered courage to tell her.

"I want to go alone and surrender to government soldiers."

Involuntarily her head jerked upward to look at him, her face tense with fear.

"Why do you want to give yourself to the soldiers? Didn't they kill our men who went to surrender? Why would they fail to kill you?"

"We do not know that they killed our men. Mother, I am weary of suffering and of being afraid. When I was in the camp of Mulele I saw something happen not once, but twice. When I arrived at the end of myself I decided to look at death eye-to-eye, and every time something good came of it. Sometimes God does not answer our prayers until He sees we are willing to lay down our lives for His answer."

She was gazing into the fire again, deep in thought. At length she spoke.

"Kimeya, once these troubles separated us. For seven long months the children and I were alone. For much of the time I was ill with worrying. At day I could not eat. At night I could not rest. When sleep did catch me I had bad dreams of how they were treating you. Then friends took us away from our home, I and the children alone. Then came my hemorrhaging problem. I endured it alone. Then I suffered on the open prairie giving birth to your children, alone. Do you know what all these things do to a person inside? Now you say you are going to give yourself into the hands of the government soldiers and leave me and the children alone. Don't do it, I beg of you."

"Then what would you like for me to do?"

"If you die, I have no way of getting to those who would help me. I don't want to die alone with the children here. Stay with us. Let the soldiers find us here. If a strange man alone goes and suddenly appears among them, they will consider him a rebel. If they come here and find a whole village of people sitting in peace, they may show us mercy."

"That would be good if it were thus," Stephen pondered. "But what if the rebels arrive first?"

She glanced at him alarmingly, then gazed into the fire's glowing embers.

"If you are really going to the soldiers, then take me and the children with you," she replied.

"No. The journey may be hard. I may need to hide waiting for the right moment to surrender. Be assured that after the soldiers have received me, I will return to get you." He did not mention the rumor that the rebels now lined this side of

224

the river and were executing anyone caught defecting to government forces.

Slowly she shook her head in refusal.

"My heart is torn with fear," she said. "You are my husband, the father of my children. If you really care for us, stay close to us."

Together they stared into the dying embers, pondering their dilemma.

"It is time to go to bed," Kimeya finally said. "First let's pray to God about this matter."

They bowed together in the darkness. Kimeya prayed.

"Father of love, You see our trouble. You have already done amazing things for us. Many times You have sent Your children to help us. Other times You bared Your own arm of might to save us. When I was captive in the camp of Mulele, You drew my attention to the Macedonian call. That gave me hope. You asked me to return to Mudidi. Then, performing a miracle, You delivered me from my captivity. That proved to me that the call came from You. It showed that You still had work for me to do. Now, after having already done all that for me, after reuniting me with my family, if You now see that it is good for me to be killed by the rebels or by the soldiers, if You, a Father of love, see that it is good for my wife to remain a widow and my children orphans, that is Your business. We stand at a fork in the path. Show us which way to go. Whatever happens, may Your Son Jesus be glorified. We beg for all these matters in His name. Amen."

They entered the dark hut, closed its door, and laid down on their separate sleeping mats. A long time passed before either of them fell asleep. When the first rooster crowed Kimeya was awake. He listened as Sona and the two girls made the sounds of sleep. He rose quietly, dressed, slipped out through the door empty-handed, and left.

Chapter Eighteen

Jim Bertsche gripped the steering wheel of the loaded truck as its front tires edged their way across hard-earth anthills protruding above the improvised roadbed. His attention was fastened to the truckload of combat-ready soldiers advancing between high walls of grass just ahead of him.

It was during the dry season of 1965. Almost sixteen months had passed since he and fellow missionaries had endured sixty-eight hours of terror at Kende in the hands of invading rebels and were eventually lifted out by a United Nations helicopter. Now he was going to Kende again.

After those final climactic days at Mudidi and Kende stations, Bertsche and his family had relocated eastward across the Loange River to the station where Elder Kalau subsequently led the Bible Institute families to refuge. Bertsche had been following events of the revolution with intense interest. The same was true of fellow missionaries and black Christians living all along the perimeter of the strife-torn region. Their primary sources of information were rumors which filtered out of the region, news brought them by Missionary Aviation Fellowship pilots flying over the region, and reports brought out by escapees.

During the past three months word had leaked out of a growing rift between the rebel leadership and people living in the area of Mudidi. Then came successive rumors of resistance by Chief Mazemba's people, reprisals taken against them, executions, and eventually fierce battles. Missionary pilots flew over the locality to check out rumors and brought information confirming them: Mudidi station and its adjacent villages were ransacked, burned, and abandoned. Later news came that Mudidi-area people had found haven in distant villages toward Kende.

Bertsche had frequent radio contact with a missionary living in Kikwit, the capital city of Kwilu Province. It was a river port town on the far northwestern fringe of the region affected by the revolution. Mulelist forces had launched savage attacks against government troops defending the town and had been repulsed. One day the missionary there relayed to Bertsche significant news: Military forces on the offensive had retaken Kende. Jim asked if it might be possible to travel to Kende by road. A few days later the reply came: "Military officials will allow such a trip only with an armed escort."

This news gave Jim pause for deliberation. Should he and a mission team travel with armed escort and take the risks inherent in identifying a missionary venture with the national military forces? He reviewed the objectives he hoped to accomplish by making such a trip: to learn first-hand what was actually transpiring, to demonstrate the church's ongoing concern and love for believers in the rebel-held areas by an appearance of its leaders on the scene, and to deliver supplies of food and clothing to destitute refugees escaping from these areas. He recognized that the requirement of a military escort also implied some threat to the personal safety of those involved. He decided to take the risks.

Necessary arrangements were made by radio. Ben Eidse, a missionary colleague who lived on the southern perimeter of the affected region, would drive a three-ton mission truck to Kikwit. He would bring with him Victor Bambi, a student from the same theological school, where James Ilunga and several other of the missions' pastors had trained. The young man originated from Kende. Bertsche would take Pastor David Ngolo, spiritual head of the conference of churches of the entire mission area, who lived on the station with him. The two of them would fly to Kikwit to join Eidse and Bambi. There the team of four would load the truck with relief supplies, meet their military escort, and leave for Kende.

This was the second day of a grueling, nerve-wracking trip. There was an army truck ahead of him and one behind him. Each of them was loaded with weapons, munitions, and about fifteen helmeted soldiers armed with rifles, machine guns, side arms, and grenades. The trail was already worn by military convoys that had used it in recent weeks. Periodically, there was a stretch of open road where the lead truck picked up enough speed to fill the air with choking dry-season dust. Then the trail would suddenly veer to the right or left across rough open prairie and back again to detour the obstruction of a deep trench or a felled tree. Every roadside village was razed to the ground and abandoned. Soldiers were continually on the alert for an ambush.

The trip had already netted unexpected side benefits. The day before they had driven as far as Mwangu, a town with a sprawling residential quarter, small commercial enterprises and an army battalion headquarters. The mission team went to spend the night at a church-school post in charge of an African pastor. News of the mission truck's arrival spread like wildfire. Soon six men appeared. They were believers from the Mudidi area. Just the previous week they had left Chief Mazemba and his people who were residing temporarily in villages some distance from Kende. At night they had reached the river, slipped through rebel lines, and swum across. The following morning they had surrendered to army troops who then brought them to Mwangu. They had found no way of sending word back to their tribesmen.

They described how a rift had developed between the people of Mazemba and rebel leadership. They defined subsequent incidents which eventually provoked open warfare. They told of the panicked mass flight of the Mudidi population. They related the experiences of Stephen Kimeya and of other leaders, naming those who now were dead. They wondered what toll these events would exact from the church. They were dismayed by the movement's brazen flouting of moral and spiritual values they had come to cherish. They described the atmosphere of hatred, vindictiveness, betrayal and terrorism, and the widespread deprivation which now were turning masses of people against the revolution. The feelings of the group had been aptly expressed by one of them who was a teacher. He sat slumped on a step, his elbows propped onto his knees, his hands supporting his head. Shadows under his eyes spoke eloquently of the ordeal he had endured. Punctuating his words with the shaking of his head, he repeated over and over again, "We've had enough. We've had enough."

Suddenly Bertsche's attention was jerked back to the road. The truck ahead of him had stopped. Just ahead of it a sandbank rose high on either side offering perfect cover for an ambush. Soldiers with machine guns at the ready slowly crawled onto the cab roof and the sides of the steel bed, then warily rose to their full height to peer behind the sandbanks. They paused a moment, then dropped back into their places. The truck began creeping forward again.

Jim glanced at Eidse and David Ngolo alongside him. No one was in the mood for conversing. Each was lost in his own thoughts. Bertsche greatly admired Pastor David. The only son of a tribal subchief, he was converted to Christ when an adolescent. His life had been closely intertwined with that of the mission for forty years. Loyalty had been the hallmark of his Christian commitment. He had served as a goatherd, a yardman, a cook, an evangelist, a teacher, a circuit-riding preacher, and was now the elected president of the conference of churches comprising some 23,000 believers. In order to shepherd scattered flocks of believers and to preach the gospel in outlying villages of his own home area he had pedaled bicycles one after another until they were worn out.

The Loange River separated Ngolo's home area on the east from the war-ridden Kwilu Province on the west. The pastor was deeply concerned about the welfare of believers who lived west of the river and had been isolated from the rest of the church by the tragic events in Kwilu. When he learned that refugees had escaped rebel control by crossing the river and were relocating east of it, he and Bertsche took relief supplies and ministered to them. He determined by the grapevine the whereabouts of Pastor James Ilunga and he sent an undercover messenger west across the river deep into rebel-held territory with an appeal for Ilunga to come out to freedom. The messenger delivered the message and returned. James Ilunga had not yet appeared. Bertsche was certain that Pastor David Ngolo would continue to play a central role in this unfolding drama.

At about noontime a familiar landscape caught Jim's attention. Kende Station was less than a mile away. The lead vehicle turned left into another detour trail. Jim braked the truck, shifted down, and slowly followed. He felt mounting excitement about what they would find. Nostalgic memories flooded across the screen of his mind: classrooms full of happy, chattering children — the church packed for weddings, graduations, holiday festivals — his home with its warmth and security. Bumps in the winding trail jerked the steering wheel. The truck body twisted and groaned as if to complain. They followed the trail as it eventually meandered back toward the right. Then, abruptly, they found themselves on the edge of Kende Station.

Along the left side of the road Bertsche saw about eight grass huts. Apparently they provided shelter for the military garrison now stationed here. A black man in civilian clothes emerged from a hut and approached the caravan. Jim stopped the truck. He and his colleagues dismounted to introduce themselves.

"Hello," the man said, reaching for a handshake. "I am a government agent."

Jim shook the man's hand. "We are from the

Protestant Mission which has been working in this region," he said. He introduced himself and each of his colleagues by name. "My family and I were living here when the rebels burned the station in January of 1964. These men have worked for the church for years; they know many of the local people here. We have come to learn what the situation is."

"The situation is improving," the agent reported. "The army offensive is progressing. Troops have already crossed Kende River. Soldiers who arrived with you in these trucks are going to reinforce them."

Bertsche noticed that the soldiers, carrying backpacks, boxes of ammunition, and mortar launchers, were already on their way east down the path toward the river.

"We had hoped to reestablish contact with people from here," he said. "We have brought food and clothing to help them."

"My assignment here is to rehabilitate refugees as they come out of the forest," the agent explained. "Soldiers across the river keep sending appeals for them to surrender, but to the present only about a dozen have responded." He gestured down the row of huts. Jim noticed a scattering of dispirited emaciated persons in tatters sitting on the ground outside the two end grass shelters. He recognized none of them.

"Have you any word about where the people of Kende are hiding?" Jim asked.

"Yes, we know where they are. We also know

the location of Paul Lamba who was a pastor here at Kende. He is in charge of a large number of refugees from his home village. However, soldiers are ordered to not press their offensive toward such places. To do so would provoke unnecessary killing. We know people will begin coming out when they are ready."

"Have you heard any word about Stephen Kimeya? He has worked as a school director for the mission for many years. We think he is sitting with the refugees from Mudidi."

"No," the man said, shaking his head thoughtfully. "We have heard nothing about him."

"We assured the commandant in Kikwit that we would return with the convoy tomorrow," Bertsche explained. "Do you know of others who might give us information on what is happening to the people from Kende?"

"There is a small village down the path toward the river. It was not destroyed. People have returned to reoccupy it. You might go ask them. However, you must not go beyond it. You may go anywhere you please on the site of Kende village and the mission station. But first, I need to enter your names into my register."

The four men separately repeated their names. Having finished with formalities, they thanked the agent and ate a lunch of stale bread and canned sardines. Then they toured the station. There was no sign that a human being had set foot on it for months. It had apparently lain abandoned for a full cycle of seasons. They walked to the Bible Institute buildings and found only heavily-eroded red-earth walls jutting above tall, yellow stalks of dry-season elephant grass. They stepped inside a classroom where a snake slithered along the base of a wall. Nettles tore at their socks and pant legs. On one wall a scarred, weather-worn blackboard was crammed with the meaningless scrawlings of some mentally disturbed villager.

They walked past the small building housing a power plant and noticed through a gaping window the battered diesel engine sitting askew on its base. They visited a literature storeroom. A two-ton supply of books and pamphlets had been reduced by sun, wind, and rain to a pulp mat, which completely covered the floor to a depth of a couple of inches. On leaving, Jim picked up a legible fragment at the doorway and read: "Why do you call me 'Lord, Lord' and do not the things that I say?" They went to the station's oldest missionary residence, once an imposing adobe-brick structure graced on two sides by a stone-pillared veranda. Now the tall stone columns partially surrounded a huge mound of red dirt, reminding Jim of pictures he'd seen in an archeology book.

Their thinking was interrupted by the chatter of machine-gun fire and the heavy thump of exploding mortars coming from the direction of the river.

"Sounds like those soldiers have encountered resistance," Jim remarked.

"I hope it doesn't have to last too much longer," Eidse said.

They arrived at the Bertsche residence. Jim paused, sighed, and ambled through the doorless front entryway. The heat that fiery night had been so intense that the sheet aluminum roof had melted. Hardened globules of molten aluminum still clung to the walls. Stones in a fireplace facing had exploded. He kicked through the aging debris. Here was half a saucer bearing the fading picture of the city hall in Brussels, Belgium; there was the handled fragment of a bright-flowered teacup.

He glanced into what had been the office. There was the window space through which he had watched the rebels begin their attack that night. The bougainvillaea bush outside it now grew untended. From the bush a branch arched back through the window casement and now reached seven feet into the office. Loaded with brilliant lavender blossoms, it stirred in a slight breeze. From across the river came the sound of gunfire of the military patrol.

Jim walked into the kitchen. The hulk of their refrigerator lay rusting in a corner. A Pyrex measuring cup lay flattened, congealed by a fierce heat. He noticed a molten aluminum slab. A few cogs were partially embedded in it, a spring jutted from one end of it. Once it had been the gearbox of their Maytag washing machine. He picked it up to keep as a souvenir.

The four men left the house and walked toward the church. Witnessing the evidence of such wanton destruction of facilities which had brought hope and blessing to thousands of people was depressing. They entered the roofless church and found an epitaph scrawled in charcoal on a wall which indicated that someone else was more than depressed. He was bitter. "You little thieves," he had written. "Yours is a revolution of lies."

They left the church and walked to a cluster of embowering mango trees to one side of the station. Here rebels had met regularly for indoctrination and training. Beneath the trees church benches, now grayed and worn by the elements, sat in a disarranged circle. A light pole had been transplanted from the station to the center of the circle to serve as a flagpole. Nearby they found a double row of charred stick stumps protruding through black grass ash — the remains of shelters used by the rebels prior to the military attack.

The men headed back to their truck. It was late afternoon now. They opened cans of food, heated them on an outside fire, and ate supper. They set up camp cots in a grass hut and put things in order for the night. Then about sundown, they walked toward the river to visit people in the reoccupied village. The people were jubilant to see them. An old villager beaming a toothless smile, reached out his hands to greet them.

"Thank you, God! Thank you, God! Truly God does exist!" he exclaimed, energetically pumping the hands of each of them in turn. "None of us believed that we would ever see the face of one of our white preachers again."

Hurriedly villagers found things for the guests to sit on. Then seven older village men joined them in a tight circle around an outside fire and began answering questions. Yes, they had been the first to respond to the call of the government to come out; that was two weeks ago. No, they had not come from across Kende River; they had been hiding in a nearby forest. Yes, they heard that the rebels were killing people for nothing. When someone was caught trying to escape, he was tied hand and foot and thrown into the river. No, the government military had not taken reprisals against them; they had come out as a village group. They knew the region where Chief Mazemba and the people of Mudidi were sitting. Villages there were small and few and the rebels had not yet claimed authority over the region. People from the mission and the villagers of Kende were hiding at one place in the forest. Yes, they knew the exact location. No, none of those people had come out yet. All the refugees must be suffering much hunger now because they are so many and fields are so few. Pastor James Ilunga and the men nurses who guarded the missionaries in the hospital had entered into the movement; no one knows where they are now. That person Mulele and his helpers have made the land very sick. Everybody wishes they would die so that the suffering would end. The village men were voluble; they seemed to find a catharsis for their bitterness in the flow of words. They talked with their visitors for two hours. Finally Bertsche and his colleagues said goodbye and began wending their way through the darkness up the hill toward the grass hut where they were to spend the night.

Jim found little new information in what the men had shared. Nevertheless, he was glad for the contact. These men claimed no particular allegiance to Christ or to the church. They were ordinary village people. In all probability the attitudes expressed here were a microcosm of those shared by village people in general. He wondered what his colleagues were thinking.

"How do you feel about all that we've heard today?" Bertsche asked.

"People are disgusted with this revolution business," Pastor David Ngolo observed. "They are turning against it."

"How much longer will it be until the business is finished?" Jim asked.

"The rebels who have given their whole heart to the movement will keep on fighting until they are all dead. They will hide in the forest and cause trouble for a long time. But the people have rejected them."

"But don't you see the trouble our people will suffer until they break free from the rebels?" interjected the young man Bambi. "How many more must die until that day comes?"

It took a few moments for someone to formulate an answer. There was only the sound of their walking.

"It is not for us with our human minds to measure such things," Ngolo, the veteran pastor replied. "We can only rest in what we read from the Book of God. It says that God is a righteous judge. He preserves the souls of His saints. The death of one of them is precious in His sight. He has not abandoned His children. He knows what He is doing. There is a proverb which says, 'The Great Elder Spirit, doing bit by bit, always succeeds. Look at the tiny termite; little by little even it eats a house.' "

There was silence as the men pondered these words. At the appropriate moment Bertsche spoke again.

"Pastor Ngolo, if you are correct in saying that people have rejected the movement, then they will begin coming out of the forest to surrender to the government soldiers."

"They will start coming soon. They will come by the hundreds and thousands."

"What should we be doing now to prepare ourselves to help them?"

"My thoughts have already entered that path," Ngolo responded. "Did not the words of those men this evening reveal their bitterness? For many months now people have suffered at the hands of the jeunesse. Many of them are our Christians. They live in the forest or high grass like animals. They have watched their children die from disease or from lack of food. They have

241

watched loved ones beaten or executed. Is it surprising that they are bitter? Do you think they are able to love their enemies? Many of our Christians have failed because of all that has happened. They carry heavy burdens. They have stumbled. The hearts of some are reeking with sin. They don't know what to do about it. We have a great debt toward them. When we receive word that they are coming out in great numbers, we need to plan another trip. We will bring them food and clothing for their bodies and we will also preach to them the Word of God to heal their souls."

Other members of the team were enthusiastic about the idea.

"What else can we do on this present trip?" Bertsche asked.

"There is not much else we can do because we did not find people from Kende as we had hoped," mused Bambi.

"We brought clothing, and blankets, and canned meat to give to the refugees," missionary Eidse observed. "There is no point in returning home with them. Tomorrow morning let's give things to the few refugees who have already come out and leave what remains with the government agent. He can distribute them to other refugees who will be coming out later."

The men reached their hut and turned in for the night. Next morning by ten o'clock, a few more refugees had arrived. They could not furnish the visitors any additional information. Military personnel began preparing their two trucks for the return trip. Bertsche and his colleagues distributed relief goods to the refugees who were present; a much larger quantity remained, which they left with the government agent.

Armed troops returning to Mwangu climbed into the trucks and the convoy re-formed to begin the slow, tension-freighted return trip. As the mission truck began to lurch and bounce its way back over the meandering detour path, Bertsche began to evaluate their experience.

Just what had they accomplished by coming at this time? True, they had realized their basic objectives. But they had seen no leaders or Christians from the Kende locality. Was timing of the trip premature, or of the Lord? Viewing again the devastation of the compound had been unnerving. More importantly, what devastation had the insurrection wreaked on the church? He had found little information to answer that question.

Still he was convinced that if the trip was no more than a gesture, it had been profitable. While they were distributing relief supplies to those few refugees, a man was heard to remark to a bystander, "Today we have seen real men of God. We burned their houses down over their heads and today they return to give us gifts to help us in our sufferings." The gesture would be understood not only by ordinary village people, but also by the rebels who controlled them. Moreover, unknown to Bertsche, the fate of both

Kimeya and Lamba would hinge on this trip.

Jim was confident that the African grapevine would serve them well. News of the team's visit was already speeding in all directions. His imagination filled in the picture. The news would spark incredulity and then joy: "People from the church and mission — people whom we offended and harassed and tormented — people whose property we destroyed — they came looking for us? They brought food and clothing for us? They will forgive us? They are ready to receive us?" Pastor David Ngolo was right. People were sick of the hunger and enmity and strife and dying. Soon they would be coming. They would come by the hundreds and thousands.

Chapter Nineteen

Stephen Kimeya edged ahead, making one step and then another, warily, fearfully. The sun was well up in the sky on the second day of his journey. It was a perilous journey. The terrain was somewhat unfamiliar to him. And he remembered the rebel stratagems. As a secretary at Mulele's camp he had read them so many times that he had memorized them. For the full distance he had been praying, "Lord of hosts, surround me with angels bearing swords of fire." Amazingly, he had met no one along the way.

He had not traveled last night. He was afraid of tripping a rebel booby trap in the darkness. He had fashioned himself a hideout in heavy underbrush and had slept on a cushion of leaves. Shortly after resuming his journey this morning he had found an abandoned village site. On it was a tree overburdened with ripening grapefruit. He had eaten two of them and slaked his thirst. He was hungry. If he understood his location correctly, he had less than an hour's walk to reach the river where he understood the rebels had their line of defense against soldiers approaching from Kende.

How would he get through that line of rebels? His anxiety heightened with every step. What if he got caught? He simply would not allow himself to think of it. Must he really go through with his plan? There was no alternative. He had promised Sona that he was going to look at death eye-to-eye. He must simply embrace the danger and trust God. Suddenly his eye caught a path overgrown from disuse which forked to the right. Before the revolution it had led to a local state post. Alongside it he saw a small crude board sign with freshly painted letters: *Military Camp*.

His mind reeled. What was a government military camp doing here? It appeared that unwittingly he had already escaped the rebels. Government troops had apparently broken the river line of defense and retaken the area. The ground he stood on was under their control.

"Well, I have arrived," he affirmed to himself. "Now what am I going to do?" He paused only momentarily and then answered himself. "I'm going into their camp and let them do with me as they wish."

He followed the forking path and soon heard the muffled sounds of drumbeating. As he approached the camp he saw the soldiers. They encircled a drummer and were dancing. He reached the edge of the clearing and stood waiting until one of them saw him and came running.

"Welcome!" he shouted.

The soldiers abandoned their dance and came rushing toward the newcomer. They led him between freshly constructed grass huts into the center of camp and pointed him to a chair.

"Sit down," they ordered.

Kimeya sat down, alerting his senses to read their moods.

One of them brought a large calabash of palm wine with an enamel cup setting upside down over its neck, and placed it on the ground before him.

"Have a drink."

Kimeya paused, then replied, "I don't drink things which intoxicate."

"You're going to drink that wine," three or four of them commanded. They stood glowering at him. He sat motionless.

There was a tap on his shoulder. He turned to see. A soldier gestured with his head toward a nearby hut and turned to go toward it. Kimeya rose and followed the man into the hut. On a table he noticed a bowl containing a round loaf of manioc mush and a small dish of greens.

"I don't know you. But the only persons who refuse to drink intoxicating things are Protestants," the stranger said. "I myself am a Protestant. I went into this soldier business only because I had no other way to make money to care for my family. But I don't want my soldier work to mess up my faith. I have no reason to take reprisal against you. I am your friend. I will intercede for you. I had fixed this food for myself when you arrived. Sit down. Eat it in peace." He turned and left.

Kimeya decided that if he were going to be executed, there was no harm in enjoying a good meal first. He ate and then returned outside.

"Who are you?" they accosted him.

"I am Stephen Kimeya."

Few heard him. They were already disputing his fate in Tshiluba, a language used east of Kwilu Province which they presumed he did not understand.

"Since we arrived we've not seen a person come to us voluntarily like this. He came empty-handed. Why would he have an evil heart toward us?" The Christian and a few others were taking his defense.

"You're wasting your time pleading for him. He's a rebel like all the rest," others countered angrily.

"But perhaps he knows something that would be of help to us. Let's question him. Why did he come? What kind of work was he doing?"

"The rebels are liars. He would tell us nothing that would help us. It would be good to destroy him."

As the debate intensified it became obvious that Kimeya's friends were outnumbered. Angry soldiers were on the point of laying hands on him.

"Why are you tormenting me?" Stephen interjected in the same language. "I am no rebel. I am a human being like you. You should know that among those hiding in the forest, all of them are not your enemies. Many of them are innocent. They were forced to help the rebels because they had no way of escaping from them. I have not come to cause you trouble. I have come seeking an end of my troubles. I want to sit quietly under the authority of the central government."

Those whose native language was Tshiluba stared in amazement.

"Listen to that!" they exclaimed. "We were about to kill a relative of ours all because of our stupid arguing!"

Others were not convinced. They clustered to one side and began talking in Chokwe, a language spoken south of Kwilu Province. Kimeya knew it also. Again the dispute became heated. Then Kimeya came to recognize one of them who was arguing for his death. He concentrated to recall the details of his previous encounter with the man. Then suddenly he spoke directly to the man in Chokwe.

"My friend, don't you remember me? You were with me in 1960. You ate at my house. You counted me a person of great value then. How is it that today when you find me in the midst of suffering, you say I am worthless?"

"You're lying. Where did I see you?"

"What did you come to my house asking for?"

The man's face wrinkled in a frown. Then it lit with recognition.

"Truly! I remember now! We came to your

249

house asking for gasoline. You gave some to us. We paid nothing for it."

The dispute dissipated.

"Who is this man, knowing all these languages?" they began asking each other.

"Someone who has been to school a lot. He must be from the mission."

"What is your name?" a man asked. Kimeya noticed on his sleeve the chevrons of a major sergeant. Everybody was listening now.

"My name is Stephen Kimeya."

"Isn't that the name of the person they said we should be looking for?" someone suggested.

The sergeant extracted a soiled notebook from his shirt pocket and began perusing its pages.

"Do you know Bertsche?" he asked.

"Yes."

"Where is he?"

"I don't know. Since this fighting started I have not seen him. But he is a missionary in our community."

"Do you know David Ngolo?"

"Yes. He is president of our conference of churches."

"Do you know Victor Bambi?"

Stephen could not believe his ears.

"Yes. Bambi was a student in theology school. He comes from Kende."

Soldiers were looking at each other, shaking their heads in bewilderment.

"What is your work?" the sergeant asked.

"I have been a director of primary schools. Because of my work I have lived in far-separated places in this part of our country. For that reason I know several languages."

"There is no doubt. He is the one they are looking for," soldiers affirmed.

"Show him a place to sleep," the sergeant ordered. "Tomorrow I'll send him to the commandant at Kende."

They took Kimeya to a grass hut and showed him an empty mat lying on the ground between the mats of other soldiers. When he lay down for the night, sleep was far from his thinking. His mind kept replaying what had happened that day. It was all too good to be true. Surely the soldiers were playing out some sort of scheme to trap him. Who was looking for him? What did they want to do with him? But no. Such thinking left too many questions unanswered.

To begin with, how had he slipped unnoticed through the rebel lines? How did those two persons, a Christian and a chance acquaintance of five years ago, happen to be in this garrison when he arrived? How did this sergeant know about his friends Bertsche and Ngolo and Bambi? Who had left word with military authorities to be on the lookout for him? All of these things were important to his escaping alive. By what means had all these things happened together? The thought sent his head swimming. All he could do was thank and praise God for heeding his prayers. Perhaps someday he would come to understand.

Kimeya began discovering the answers to

some of his questions on the following morning. Two armed soldiers took him across the river in a dugout to a military headquarters on the edge of Kende Station. There they presented him to the commandant and to a government agent dressed in civilian clothes. The two officials repeated questions asked him yesterday, thereby confirming his identity.

"We are very happy to see you," the agent said. "Your three friends came here looking for you. Inasmuch as you are a school director, we want you to stay here at Kende. Hunt for pastors and teachers and others who will help the people. Spread the word that you are organizing classes. We want to open school in September."

Stephen felt a surge of pure joy. If Kimeya's duties with the mission had been the cause of his troubles, it was now clear that his linguistic knowledge and his reputation gained in the course of those duties were the means of his salvation.

"Where are your wife and children?" the commandant asked. "I'll give you an armed soldier escort to go with you all the way to where they are so that you can bring them out. You can go tomorrow."

"It would not be good for me to return with soldiers," Kimeya replied. "My wife would not know that I was with them. If soldiers began shooting as is their custom, my wife and children would flee with everybody else. It would be better that I return alone and bring them out."

Kimeya was convinced that the angels which had surrounded him on one trip would not abandon him on another.

"No," the military officer objected. "That is too dangerous. If you refuse for soldiers to go with you, then stay here on the station. Start putting things in order to begin your work."

During the following days, a steady trickle of former Kende residents was coming from hiding. People gave themselves to building temporary shelters. Stephen borrowed a hoe and machete and cleared an area where he would build his house. He was able to recruit a few teachers. Class children, excited at the prospect of studying again, helped him gather grass and sticks. Together they built his shelter. At the end of a week he was called to the hut of the government agent. He found the agent and the military commandant seated at a table.

"Soldiers continue to make progress beyond the river," the agent announced. "They are coming near that area where your wife and children sit. The commandant feels that the danger of the rebels catching you is reduced. We are allowing you to leave for two days to go and get your family. Here is an official pass explaining the purpose of your trip. You will show it to any soldiers you may encounter."

Kimeya took the paper.

"You will leave in the morning to arrive at the village by tomorrow evening," the commandant instructed. "You will spend the night there.

Then you and your family will return all the way to here on the following day. I will be awaiting your arrival. Heed that schedule. If you have not returned by four o'clock the following morning I am sending a company of soldiers to hunt for you."

Kimeya thanked them and returned to his hut. Early the next morning he left. He walked the full distance without incident and arrived at the village in the late afternoon where he found Sona and the children in mourning. He had been gone too long, they had given up hope. He said little until that night after the children were asleep and he and Sona were to themselves inside the hut. Then he recounted to her all that had happened and shared with her the plan to leave in the morning. They were up before daybreak. While Sona prepared a full meal Stephen awakened the children and helped them get ready to leave.

"We're going on a long journey to some friends," he explained. "It will take us all day to get there. Strengthen your hearts and don't ask any questions."

They ate. Sona placed a loaf of manioc mush and a small dish of greens in a covered wicker basket to eat en route. They had prayer committing themselves to God, went outside into the gray of dawn, and closed the door of their hut behind them for a final time. Kimeya, leading his six-year-old girl with one hand and carrying the food basket with the other, started out. Sona, with the four-year-old girl tied by waist cloth to her back, followed.

They traveled seeing no one until noon. Then they stopped in the shade of a tree along the roadside to rest and eat. Suddenly they saw a youth approaching in the road. He did not seem like a rebel; empty-handed, he walked jauntily and was whistling a tune. They waited until he arrived and greeted him.

"Where are you coming from?" Kimeya asked.

"I'm coming from Kende."

"How are things there?"

"Good."

"Sit down and eat with us," Kimeya invited.

The youth nodded his appreciation, squatted by the open basket, and began to help himself.

"For what reason do you say that things are good at Kende?" Stephen asked.

"We just got news about a person who has worked with the mission for a long time. He was caught in the rebellion. But he escaped and appeared at Kende Station. He has spread the word that classes are going to start. They sent him to get his wife and children. If he doesn't arrive today soldiers are coming tomorrow to go to his village. I've already registered my name with a teacher there. I'm going to my home village to get my books."

"Father, what is he talking about?" the older girl inquired. "Is that where we are going?"

"Hush," Kimeya scolded. "Didn't I tell you not to ask questions?"

They finished eating in silence and prepared to leave.

"I am that person they are talking about," Kimeya admitted. "Go get your books and come back to study."

"Tribe mate, you did something that makes happy the hearts of all of us," the young man exulted. His spirits soaring even higher, he continued on his way.

Kimeya and his family made contact with advance military troops in midafternoon. He showed them his pass paper. They welcomed him. One soldier was assigned to accompany them across the river. The group arrived at Kende after dark and went directly to the hut of the commandant. The two children were sleeping now, the parents carrying them. Kimeya, standing at the closed door, noticed a light and heard talking inside. He knocked.

"Who is there?" It was the officer's voice.

"Me. Stephen Kimeya."

The door opened revealing the officer and half-a-dozen soldiers. They were jubilant at seeing him with his family.

"These are the men I was planning to send after you in the morning," the commandant said. "I was giving them their instructions. You are trustworthy. They won't need to go. Let's go to our places to sleep."

Carrying their girls, Kimeya and Sona wearily turned and walked into the darkness. He led her slowly along the path which took them to his new-built grass hut. His emotions were too numbed from tension and fatigue to respond to the import of the moment. They would go lie down and sleep tonight with no fears for their safety. Tomorrow they could start planning their lives together again. Soon they would resume their custom of meeting with the family of God's people to worship and to pray. Something told him that their long dark night of tribulation was finally coming to its end.

Chapter Twenty

Pastor Paul Lamba waited. Time crept by. From dawn to dusk seemed the length of an age. Why had he made the appointed date so far into the future? Every day increased the possibility that his plot would be uncovered or that his children would not survive. With the passing of each succeeding day he breathed a bit more easily and garnered a fresh measure of hope that the plan would succeed. Then suddenly, two days before the rendezvous, events exploded which threatened to ruin everything.

That morning the pastor checked his traps and delightedly brought home a large forest rodent. Generally they had their daily hot meal in the evening. This, however, was an event for celebration. Moreover, the children needed the meat. Immediately Tembo began preparing a cooked meal. About noon they ate heartily. Soon thereafter the children began to vomit wrenchingly. It was midafternoon when vomiting finally subsided and the children began to rest quietly on their mats. Lamba did not understand the reason for it.

Shortly thereafter two armed rebels suddenly appeared in the camp asking for Pastor Paul Lamba. They reached his house and gave him a folded paper. He opened it to read. It was a subpoena demanding that he come immediately to the area command headquarters of the revolution to appear before the regional president. His bones chilled with fear. Silently he began to pray and slowly regained his composure.

"What is the matter?" he asked the rebels.

"The president will tell you when you arrive," one of them replied sternly.

Lamba gazed at him questioningly.

"Right now my children are very ill," the pastor demurred. "Can I not come tomorrow morning?"

"No. Our orders are to bring you today."

He paused, his mind working desperately to find a way out of his predicament. Finally he shrugged helplessly and went into the house. Tembo was seated on the floor near the children. He squatted, put his arm around her shoulder, and explained the situation to her. For a few moments they wept silently together. Then he squeezed her shoulder, arose, and left.

He walked ahead of his rebel guards to the headquarters camp and went directly to the house of the president. The burly officer was seated behind his table just outside the door, his face somber, his forehead scar glinting in the late afternoon sun. Suddenly Lamba noticed that four armed rebels had flanked him. For a while the president engaged him in idle chit-chat which only served to heighten the suspense. Then abruptly the rebel commander looked directly at the pastor and addressed the issue:

"We have received word that you are planning to defect to soldiers of the Central Government."

Lamba's mind groped desperately for an answer.

"The person spreading any such news about me is an enemy," he replied evasively.

The rebel officer's forehead creased in a frown. His eyes fastened themselves onto Lamba like two drawn arrows.

"Tell me the truth," he said authoritatively. "Are you arranging to surrender your village people to forces of the Central Government?"

What should he answer? Thoughts raced through his mind. He feared that his word of truth would send a thousand people rushing down a river of blood to their doom. Was he obliged to tell the truth? By now he had seen supporters of the revolution scorn and desecrate all that the Bible called truth. Their conduct revulsed him. The thought of such people ruling his country terrified him. This man had lied to him the last time. These people were disciples of the devil. They were masters of deceit. They were enemies of all unrighteousness. Why should he utter truth to serve them? If he confessed, they would find him guilty of treason and execute him. They would take savage reprisal on his wife, on his children, and on his people. He was a man of compassion. What should he do? He would do what Isaac under far less duress had done long ago. He would lie. In all probability they would then beat him mercilessly in an effort to extract the truth. Those were chances he would take. He would pay any price at this point to help rescue those dear to him.

"Sir, whatever you have heard about my planning to defect to government forces is false. I know nothing about any such arrangement."

There. He had said it. He awaited their response. The air was tight as a drumhead. The rebel commander held his gaze for a moment longer and then shifted his eyes to look at the table before him.

"Shall we beat him?" a guard asked. The four of them tensed for action.

"No," the president replied. "I have confidence in this person. I have known him for a long time. Years ago I was among children who went to school at Kende Station. I remember the preaching of this man. He insisted that we always be truthful. He punished students who did not tell the truth. Would the man who has spent all the years of his life teaching people to speak truth lie to me today? I accept his word."

Then he addressed himself to Lamba:

"Pastor, I want to warn you that during these days the leaves of the trees have ears. Don't say anything which will suggest that you are collaborating with our enemies. You may go."

Half in a daze, the pastor thanked the rebel commander, shook hands with him, and left. Inside he was torn by conflicting emotions. On the one hand he felt jubilant, for it looked as though he and his people were going to be liberated after all! On the other hand he felt shame. He was betraying a man's trust. There was even the fleeting thought that perhaps he should not go through with the plan to prove to the rebel commander that he *was* a man of integrity. But no — his children were ill and needed help. Neither was it fair to prolong the tribulation of a thousand people in respect to his compassion for one man.

He slept little that night — or the night following. These portentous events laid claim to his mind. On the day of the planned encounter he stayed for the morning worship service so as to not arouse suspicion. Afterwards, he did not wait to eat. Wearing his fraying white shirt and a loincloth, he took nothing in his hands, and left. He followed the path which led toward their abandoned village site, greeting an occasional sentry he met along the way. When he reached the village, its utter desolation and the eerie silence steeped him in melancholy. Would the day ever come when people would live here again, when the air would carry the odor of cooking fires and the voices of happy children? He wandered slowly past the empty houses. Then he walked up the road, rounded the bend, and reached the tall nsanga tree. He slipped to the back side of it and flattened coarse grass beneath overarching brush to make a den in which to conceal himself. There he sat to wait.

The waiting was almost unbearable. It seemed the sun stood still in the sky. Would the soldiers really come looking for him? How would they receive him? What manner of entry into the refugee camp would provoke a minimum of disorder? Would the soldiers shoot? Would any of his people die? During the course of waiting he must have asked himself these questions a hundred times. At what points might the plan take an unexpected shift in direction? What should be his course of action if any such changes should happen?

The sun was well past its zenith when his ears picked up the indistinct sound of a motor. He stopped breathing and strained to hear. Yes, it was unmistakable. A truck was approaching. His heart began to pound. Was it possible that the truck might be loaded with rebels? No. This sounded like a big truck. He had heard no rumor that insurgents were in possession of large trucks. How should he make his appearance? Should he wait until the truck rounded the bend to make sure it was government soldiers and then suddenly jump into the road? No. Soldiers would be tensed, prepared for an ambush. If he appeared abruptly, they might shoot him. The motor noise was loud now, they must be passing the village.

"Oh my God," he pleaded. "I put myself into Your hands. Please have mercy on us."

He emerged from his hideout, stood on the edge of the road in full view, held his hands high to show that he offered no resistance, and waited. A truck rounded the bend. It was full of government soldiers! Following it came a second one! They cut their speed and braked to a stop, the right-hand cab door of the first truck coming abreast of him.

"Greetings!" he shouted. "I am Pastor Paul Lamba."

The soldier in the cab did not respond. He opened the door. Carefully handling a heavy rifle to avoid bumping it, he got out. On his sleeve Lamba noticed the chevrons of a master sergeant.

"Get in," the man ordered.

Lamba started. "But what about all the people who are in the forest?" he protested.

"We have orders to take you back to camp," the sergeant said curtly.

"But the rebels, what will they do when they hear. . . ."

"Get in!" the soldier cut him off. "Shall we take you by force?"

Reluctantly, fearfully, Pastor Paul Lamba complied. Where were they going with him? What did they want to do with him?

The incident did not pass unobserved. Upon hearing the approaching roar of the trucks, one of a pair of sentries from the refugee camp had climbed into a tree; though he was beyond hearing distance, he had seen it all.

"Soldiers captured pastor!" he whispered excitedly to his comrade on the ground below. "They went with him!"

The second sentry raced to relay the news. The news sped down the line of sentries and reached camp. It moved down the lines of huts like murmuring wind. Tembo, sitting on the earthen floor of her house beside her children, heard it muttered outside by an excited passerby. Her husband's arrest and interrogation by the rebel commander and her ordeal with the children had so numbed her emotions that she hardly responded. Most men were away searching for food. Christian women dispersed throughout the camp dropped the work they were doing, left infants in the care of older children or swept them onto their hips, and came running to the house of Pastor Lamba. They went inside and huddled themselves around Tembo. None of them could touch the depth of her grief. But they could empathize with her. They sang a traditional song of mourning, their bodies swaying together with its rhythm. One woman extemporized verses lauding Tembo's husband, then others chanted the refrain. Through this singing of songs and hymns, they comforted her.

On the following day when the sun had reached the middle of the sky, Tembo and her attendants were startled by noise outside. A ruckus of jabbering swelled to a jubilant crescendo. A neighbor lady popped her head into the doorway.

"Tembo," she said. "Come outside and see."

Tembo and her friends hurried from the house. Over the heads of an excited gathering crowd she discerned the face of Lamba. On his head was a bill cap. He was beaming. She ran and forced her way through the crowd to reach him. She couldn't believe her eyes. Her husband was wearing a complete outfit of clothing: a fresh white shirt, a coat, trousers, and shoes. He was raising his hands to silence the people.

"Hello there! Hello!"

The noise subsided and stopped. People waited breathlessly.

"God has done a surprising thing! When soldiers met me along the roadside they caught me. Fear gripped me. It shriveled up my insides. They took me back to their post. But when we got there, everybody rejoiced to see me.

" 'Come with us to Kende Station!' the soldiers said. 'We were with your missionary Bertsche there! He brought a big truck loaded with things: seeds, food, blankets, clothing. He was looking for you!'

"I knew my ears were lying to me. Soldiers put me into the truck and we began the journey. I asked the one sitting beside me, 'Why are you saying such things? Where are you taking me?

Are you going to kill me?' He said, 'We have no mind to kill you. We are telling you the truth. We want to save you.'

"When we arrived at the mission, a horde of soldiers came running to welcome me. 'Hello, pastor,' they were shouting. 'Life to you!' 'We rejoice for you.' 'Everybody has been hunting for you!' 'You have done well to come; you might have died for nothing in the forest.' Then a small group of church people came running, people I used to shepherd at Kende. 'Our pastor! Our pastor!' they cried. 'He was dead. He has come to life again!'

"Then the soldiers took me into a house and closed the door. I still could not believe it. What did they want to do with me now? They looked at my loincloth and began shaking their heads. They said, 'We are ashamed, pastor, that someone important like you is dressed like that.' Then they started giving me clothes. They gave me these that I'm wearing. When they opened the door and let me outside I was beaming smiles. I was laughing with joy. I was praising God. Then I began saying to myself, 'Look how happy our brothers and sisters are here! We have been torturing ourselves pointlessly out there in the jungle.'

"Then a government agent came to see me," Lamba continued. "He was not wearing a uniform like the soldiers. He said that it was his work to welcome people who were coming out of the forest. He gave them clothing and blankets and he helped them become established in their homes again. He asked what I could do to bring the refugees out of the forest camp so that he could help them. I told him I would go back myself and bring them out; I would bring them all out to their village. The man put dried fish and clothing and blankets into an army truck. Soldiers got into it and came back with me to our village. They are waiting for you there."

Refugees looked at one another unbelievingly and then looked back at the pastor.

"What an amazing affair!" they exclaimed to each other.

"Only God could do this!"

"Clansmen, are we going to stand here pointlessly talking about it?"

"Let's go to the village. Let's go, ALL of us."

News had sped along the sentry lines into all directions and people were returning from outlying areas to the camp. Paul Lamba felt no need to wait for them. In a short time he was returning along the path which led in the direction of the village. He carried his son piggyback, the boy's legs cradled loosely across his arms, the boy's bony arms tightly encircling his neck. Tembo was directly behind him, carrying their daughter in similar fashion. He knew that the path stretching behind him was full of people. He walked for a while, then paused momentarily and turned to look. He witnessed a spectacle he would never forget.

A long line of haggard weary creatures

stretched back through the enveloping dust of mid-dry season for as far as he could see. Women with rags hanging onto their bony frames carried anemic potbellied children astride their hips. Men with loin coverings of tattering cloth or gunny sack, or even of leaves, carried older emaciated children on their backs. Stronger children, naked, walked. The aged — some pulling themselves forward with walking sticks shiny with wear — others supported on either side by stronger persons, deliberately inched their way ahead step by step. The faces of many were gaunt and angular, their eyes were sunken. Lamba blinked back the tears. His heart welled with pity. These were his people. He loved them. He had suffered with them. He had risked his life to save them. What was happening was almost too good to be true. He was leading them from their long night of darkness into the light of day.

They arrived at the village where the soldiers had swept out their homes, had cleaned up debris in their yards, and were waiting for them. By sundown people had filled the village to overflowing. Soldiers parceled out dried fish, clothing, and blankets. At first people were incredulous; then they were exuberant with joy. After nightfall the soldiers brought out drums and led the refugees in a traditional dance of celebration. Hour after hour the pounding of drums and the shouts of joy reverberated through the forest. Then the rebels began to appear, timid, fearful, empty-handed. They wanted to surrender. Through the hours of the night their number grew. By morning it appeared that rebel resistance in the entire region was capitulating.

The fast-paced sweeping events of recent days had not allowed Pastor Lamba time to think. But now that responsibility for the welfare of his people was off his shoulders, he began to hear the protesting voice of conscience. For all the years of his adult life he had followed Jesus. He had sought to be faithful to God. He had taught people to forsake their sin-way of living and to obey the Bible. Now he himself had failed. He had lied. His people did not know it. But he did. The memory of that fact began to haunt him. It eroded his joy.

The memory was the more painful because he had lied to one who had trusted him. It was clear that his teaching had once made a profound impression on the regional president. Now that the entire camp population had defected to government forces, the rebel leader knew that Lamba had lied to him. What was the president's opinion of Lamba now? "I had hoped that these pastors were truly men of God," Lamba could almost hear the disillusioned man say. "But they will lie just like anybody else if they think it might save their lives." Lamba had betrayed the man's confidence. What effect would this have on the rebel leader's opinion of the Christian faith? What bearing might it have on the man's eternal salvation? Perhaps the rebel commander had been lenient in dealing with Lamba because he secretly hoped that Lamba might help him find a way out of his own dilemma. But such hope had now disappeared, for Lamba probably would never see him again. And the mass defection of rebel forces following the liberation of the camp now put the rebel leader's life in great jeopardy. Pastor Paul Lamba's spirit slipped into a dark period of despair.

Had it been necessary for him to lie? His mind searched for an answer. Yes, one part of him concluded; it was the only way that the camp of refugees could be saved. Then his mind recalled that occasion when the refugee sentry had related to him the story of Pastor Thomas Sangu. Thomas had insisted that his only "gun" was his Bible. He had stood firmly, unshakable as a boulder. The rebels had beat him, soldiers had beat him, but he had not budged. Consequently he had left a credible witness with both the insurrectionists and the government forces. And withal, he had still liberated a great number of people. The knowledge of that pastor's faithfulness now only served to aggravate Lamba's pain.

"My God, don't forsake me because of my sin," he prayed desolately. "Don't turn Your back on me forever."

He decided to return to Kende Station. He had discharged his responsibility to the people of his home village. Outwardly his people acclaimed him as their hero, but inwardly he felt like a traitor. He longed to rejoin the believers he had shepherded for so long at Kende. They were few in number now, but he was certain more would be coming. Perhaps he would find solace there. Also, his fields were there and he could find more help for his ailing children.

Just after dark on the day following their liberation Lamba went to the commanding officer of the company temporarily living in the village to make travel arrangements for himself and his family. He arrived to overhear the report of a squad which had just returned from a foray into the jungle to eliminate the rebel resistance. The leader was excitedly describing their success. The pastor listened to the chronicle for a while and then suddenly perked his ears.

"Then we found a small village on the edge of the forest," the voice was saying. "It looked like a rebel headquarters. We opened fire. The rebels began fleeing. We killed most of them, including the man we think was their leader. He was wearing an army jacket. He was a big man, with a scar on his forehead."

Inwardly Lamba reeled under the impact of the words. He felt grief edging up his throat to choke him.

"Oh God," he prayed silently. "I fear the blood of that man is on my hands."

Chapter Twenty-one

The final weeks of a tropical dry season are long and dreary. The earth underfoot, covered by a thickening blanket of dust and accumulating fragments of garbage and excrement, finally succumbs to hibernation. All of the vegetation wears the pallor of dust, its branches seem bowed with the burden of long waiting, its leaves bravely hold their brown dust-laden faces upward hoping to be washed. The canopy of heaven itself seems to protest against the volume of polluting elements it must bear, blotting out the sun and pressing itself against the earth as if to suffocate all living things.

At last, those weeks had dragged to their end. Heaven burst with a deluge of rain and all of earth resounded its praise. Pigs, grunting their gratitude, trotted toward puddles to wallow. Chickens scratched the moist ground with renewed vigor in search of juicy morsels. The landscape glistened with fresh greenness, the ocular definition of its verdure leaping forth with stark and clear intensity. The air was fresh and clean. Heaven's canopy, magnanimous and forgiving,

273

was now a field of pure deep azure adorned with cotton clouds of dazzling white.

Another such day would soon dawn on Kende mission station. David Ngolo, the seasoned pastor who had accompanied James Bertsche on that memorable journey to war-ravaged Kende, had returned. He had been sleeping in one of a cluster of huts in the compound of the commanding officer of troops headquartered there. Sleeping with Ngolo were four students from the mission's theological training school, one of several teams of students who had come to minister to groups of population at scattered points now under army control. Missionary Bertsche could not make the trip, he was away with his family on vacation.

The thunderclap of a predawn shower had awakened Pastor David. Now he lay awake in the dark pondering a different storm, one which had been battering Kwilu Province for some twenty months. By now it had left the church as strewn pieces of debris. He was spiritual head of the churches of the mission's entire field. From the outset he had been deeply concerned for believers in this violence-torn region. Now his mind began to look for signs of progress they had made toward putting the battered pieces together again.

He recalled the previous trip he had made with Bertsche and the student Victor Bambi. At the time they had wondered if the trip had been premature, its results seemed so limited. Now it appeared that the timing had been arranged of God. The relief supplies brought for distribution at that time had alleviated human suffering and had proved the key factor in beginning to lure people from under rebel control, which was the first step toward restoring peace.

Some weeks after that first trip a group of theological students had accompanied a truckload of relief supplies coming to Kende. Insurgents were still firmly in control of the region. Most people were still hiding in the forest. While the vast majority of ordinary village people abhorred the rebel rule, they were also fearful of treatment they might receive at the hands of military forces if they surrendered. The students were allowed to stay for only a few days. But the impact of their witness had been far-reaching.

The truck had brought medicines, blankets, dried milk, clothing, and Bibles. The students found that Kimeya, Lamba, and Lamba's people had just recently come out of the forest. They were able to furnish them desperately needed material aid. Then students established a liaison between military forces and the fearful people still in hiding. From Kende and from nearby abandoned village sites to which soldiers escorted them, they surreptitiously contacted Christians informing them of their presence and assuring them safety if they surrendered. Each evening the students held an open-air worship service in a different village. People hiding in surrounding thickets perked their ears to hear what they had not heard for months: the lusty singing of Christian hymns. Secretly they began to steal away from rebel custody and flee in the direction of Kende.

During those few days of encounter students spent most of their time trying to contact refugees in hiding; and distributing material aid. But they quickly recognized that Christians emerging from this night of tribulation were also spiritually famished.

"Great numbers of people will soon be coming out of the forest," the students had reported upon returning home. "After some weeks we must plan another trip. We must prepare to stay a longer time to help people in their faith. Their thinking is confused. They carry great burdens of guilt. They are like sheep without a shepherd. We need to show them how they can return to the Savior."

On that same occasion another team of students had been able to travel in a military convoy to Mudidi Station. Later they had given Pastor Ngolo a detailed report. Chief Mazemba and his people were there. The despairing chief had decided to lead his people from their place of hiding back home to die. En route he was persuaded to attempt reconciliation with government forces by appealing for their help in recovering his area from the hands of the Mulelists. The commanding officer responded favorably to his appeal. The combined forces had approached Mudidi, launched an offensive, and regained control of Mudidi Station and its immediate environs. But the rebel forces continued a constant threat. They had allowed few people to slip from their grasp. Only recently Chief Mazemba and a squad of soldiers were ambushed along the main road leading from the station. The chief, his son, and a soldier had sustained flesh wounds.

"The storm there has not yet abated," Pastor Ngolo contemplated painfully. "How much longer must people bear its anger?"

He returned his thinking to Kende where the picture was brighter. This was the trip the theology students said must be arranged. He had come with them. They hoped to be used of God for spiritual revival. They had arrived the day before in the afternoon which was Saturday. During the remaining hours of the day he had visited briefly with Lamba, Kimeya, and others. What these people shared with him disclosed how the storm had affected Christian believers.

There were heroes. Two teacher-evangelists, with loaded rebel guns at their heads, refused to join the insurrection and miraculously were spared. A zealous lay preacher had refused to be silenced and bore on his body the marks of the beatings he survived. A husband and wife, when denied their right to public worship, went daily to a secret place, retrieved their hidden Testament and hymnal, and worshiped together.

There were failures. A few church leaders, initially convinced that the revolution was a positive reform movement, had continued to unswervingly defend it. Some professing Christian teachers had renounced their faith and indoctrinated believers to exhibit loyalty to the revolution. A "Christian" businessman, under the duress of torture at rebel hands, joined the cause and became notorious for his atrocities.

There was tragedy. After Bertsche's visit to Kende, the man who had once worked in Bertsche's home got word of it. He slipped out of the rebel zone and came to Kende to verify the truth of the rumor. Then, over the protests of friends, he returned to the rebel zone. The insurgents executed him. They also executed his uncle and two brothers, accusing them of complicity.

These events had occurred in the eye of the storm. Pastor David Ngolo hoped that the peak of the storm had now passed. His present concern was the inner turmoil which had begun to surface in its wake.

Many people were suffocating beneath a black cloud of guilt so oppressive that they despaired of even seeking forgiveness. Others had been so buffeted by crosscurrents of perplexity that they were on the verge of abandoning their faith. Others were tormented with hot swirling winds of resentment, accusation, bitterness, and enmity which had been triggered by misconduct one toward another during times of stress. Could the Holy Spirit of God possibly heal and restore such a deeply troubled people? Pastor David

Ngolo knew that this was the most crucial need of all in the process of piecing the church back together again.

Soon after daybreak Ngolo unfolded himself off his short sleeping mat, stood, and stretched his slender frame to its full height. He dressed and went outside into the fresh-wet world. He dashed cold water onto his face, scrubbed his teeth with the frazzled end of a short fibrous stick, and pulled a bamboo-prong comb through his kinky gray-flecked hair. Then he sat outside the hut in a worn wicker armchair to wait for a breakfast cup of tea. After drinking it he settled back in his chair to plan the morning worship service. It was scheduled to begin at nine o'clock, for an early start meant they could finish before the heat of the day. Kimbody, a third-year student with the gifts of compassion and zeal, would preach. Ngolo gripped a stub pencil in his slender fingers and thoughtfully outlined an order of worship onto a scrap of paper. He was drawing a hand across his lean cheek in contemplation of his work when suddenly Kimbody arrived.

"Pastor," he said, "don't you think we had better start the service?"

Ngolo looked at his watch. It was eight o'clock.

"Why?" he asked.

"Because all the people have already arrived. They have filled the church full. Others are sitting on the ground outside."

Ngolo got up and walked around the corner of the hut to see. It was true.

"Let's go," he replied.

Kimbody turned and left. Pastor Ngolo stepped inside the hut, picked up his Bible, and followed. They approached the roofless chapel, circled around the crowd of people sitting on the ground outside it, and reached a back door. The two men paused. A crowd of people, sitting on the bare concrete floor packed like grasshoppers in a basket, must have numbered six hundred. Kimbody and Ngolo edged their feet between human bodies and slowly made their way to the platform. People crowded together to make space for Kimbody to stand on the platform and for Pastor Ngolo to sit on its edge. Kimbody raised his arm, to silence the people. Instantly there was a hush and he began to speak.

"We have come to worship with you, just like we used to do. I read to you from the Book of God: 'If we confess our sins, He [that is, Jesus Christ the Son of God] is trustworthy, and He has the goodness to cover from sight all of our sins, and to cleanse us from all kinds of evil'. In these words our Savior promises His pardon. These words show us that we can trust Him. It makes no matter what kinds of evil we have done, He still loves us. He still counts us people of worth. His measure of goodness is so great that it will wipe out our sins. He is still your friend. He is calling you to come. He wants you to ask Him for pardon."

Kimbody was interrupted when someone began singing "What a Friend We Have in Jesus." The crowd quickly picked up the tune. They sang one verse after another from memory. They sang with deep emotion, with slow cadence, as if to draw from each passing word the sweetness of its meaning. As soon as the song ended someone else began a second one. The multitude of voices swelled it into a corporate plea of contrition:

Draw us nearer, Jesus Son of God;
Draw us nearer, by the power of Your blood.

When the last plaintive strains of the song faded, Kimbody continued:

"You suffered surpassingly in the forest. Those sufferings deranged you. You did things which sadden the Savior. Now you have received food and clothing. The suffering of your bodies has ended. But the suffering of your souls remains. The weight of the wrong things you have done surpasses your strength to carry. Don't look for forgiveness in Kimbody or in Pastor Ngolo. We are only people, like you. Forgiveness is in Jesus. If you refuse to believe these Words from God, there is nowhere else where you can find forgiveness. There is nowhere else where you can leave your burden. Come with it to Jesus. Leave it at His feet. Start talking to Him now. Tell Him. . . ."

Suddenly a man left of center in the crowd

stood and began crying out his prayer of confession. Ngolo recognized Stephen Kimeya. The man's voice was broken with contrition, his upturned face was streaming tears. He had hardly begun when a bulky man just to the right of Pastor Ngolo rose and lifted his voice in a plea for mercy. The man was Pastor Paul Lamba. Then, like random sprouts across a brown field, people cropped up and audibly began pouring out their hearts to God. Ngolo's ear picked up fragments of what they were confessing: theft, betrayal, murder. . . .

Then suddenly it happened. The power of the Holy Spirit descended upon them. Almost simultaneously a crowd of people rose to their feet as if dams of self-restraint had broken and waters of confession poured through. In a moment, each person, oblivious to all around him, was in earnest communion with his God. The sound of voices swelled together with the strength of a purging stream and then leveled to an even-flowing sustained cascade of harmony. Overcome, Pastor Ngolo felt a sob catch in his throat. He bowed his head and let the tears flow freely. He wept for his people and also for his own sinfulness.

The order of worship was abandoned. Each person prayed until he found catharsis and then quietly sat down. Someone started singing another hymn and the audience joined in. At the close of the hymn a few people were still standing in prayer. Young Kimbody cast a glance of perplexity toward David Ngolo. Pastor Ngolo rose to his feet and spoke.

"The Spirit of God has touched all of us. We have received what we all longed for. Those of you who want to talk with us may remain. The rest may leave. Go in peace."

The audience sat motionless.

"Do you understand?" the pastor asked. "The meeting is finished. You may leave."

"Pastor," a man said rising to his feet. "Our meeting was good. We encountered God. But we aren't leaving. If a person is bowed down with carrying a load for a long time, when the load is taken from him, does he stand straight up immediately? We are all staying because we want to talk with our Speakers from God. Our burden has lightened, but we still need your help to stand up straight."

People across the audience nodded their heads and grunted affirmingly.

"Fine," the pastor replied. "If that is what you want, let us begin our work. I and the preacher students who came with me will go outside and sit each at a different place in the yard, you can begin coming to us one at a time."

People formed into orderly lines and patiently waited their turns for help. The counselor sat some distance from the head of his line to respect each person's right to privacy. Among the first standing in the line before Pastor David Ngolo were Stephen Kimeya and Paul Lamba.

Kimeya squatted himself onto a chunk of firewood as a seat and looked at the pastor.

"First I want to thank you and Bertsche for coming to hunt for us," he began. "The word you left with the government agent saved my life."

Ngolo could only breathe his thanks to God.

"I felt very badly about the things which I broadcasted over the radio in the name of Mulele," Kimeya confessed quietly. "I know God has forgiven me of that and of all the wrong things I did during those months of tribulation. I have peace in my heart. Only one thing still bothers me. During the early days of the revolution one of the teachers I supervised at Mudidi betrayed me. He lied about me to Mulele hoping I would be killed. His plot failed. Now I see him walking around here at Kende. His countenance shows me that he is carrying a heavy burden. He is ashamed to come and talk to me. I feel sad for him. What can I do about it?"

"Have you forgiven him in your heart?"

"I have forgiven him. I wish he would accept my forgiveness. He is carrying his burden for nothing."

"Why don't you go and talk to him? Tell him that it makes no difference what his thinking is toward you, for you have forgiven him. God has given you peace about the affair. You love the man like you love everybody else."

"I can do that," Stephen said thoughtfully.

"Now I have a word," the pastor interjected.

"What is it?"

"Chief Mazemba of Mudidi still has bad

thinking toward you. How do you feel about him?"

Kimeya's face registered disaffection at the mentioning of the chief's name.

"I have no conflict with him," Kimeya replied. "I don't hate him."

"I want to warn you, my friend," the pastor counseled. "Do not harbor a grudge against him. Jesus refused to harbor ill will toward those who persecuted Him. When He was on the cross, those who tormented Him did not ask His forgiveness. Still He prayed, 'Father, forgive them; they don't know what they are doing.' Harboring ill will toward a person poisons one's insides like snake venom. You do not hate the chief. But do you love him?"

Kimeya shifted his eyes to the ground, frowned in deep thought, and then looked back at the pastor.

"What can I do?"

"You can write him a letter. Tell him that when dawn comes, people stop feeding their hearth fires. You have already forgiven him for wrongs done against you. You hold no ill feelings toward him. Ask him to forgive you any wrongs you did him. Tell him that whether he forgives you or not, you have put out your hearth fire and have discarded the ashes. You respect him as your chief and you love him just as God does."

Stephen was wrinkling his brow in thought.

"What you say is right," he conceded, nodding

his head understandingly. "I'll get to work on the matter."

They prayed together. As Kimeya left, the veteran pastor sensed deepened love and respect for the young man.

Paul Lamba came. He squatted, adjusted the piece of firewood beneath him, and sat down. He lifted his eyes longingly into the face of Pastor David Ngolo as if to affirm that he was not dreaming.

"Pastor, is that you?" he asked unbelievingly. "Is that really you?" Then he bowed his head to pray.

"Savior, when I was in the forest my mind became so mixed up that I was near believing that You no longer existed. I feared that the peace of Your Spirit had abandoned me forever. I had no hope of ever seeing this brother of mine again. Today my doubts are finished. We escaped from the forest. Your Spirit has returned inside of me. My brother sits alongside me here. Your name be glorified forever. You are alive! You are alive!"

He was silent for a moment, heaved a great sigh, and resumed his conversation.

"Pastor, don't be embarrassed with my repeating the matter. You cannot measure the joy I have in seeing you. I am like a dog who just escaped the claws of a ferocious animal in the forest and has returned to the village to rest. Because of the strife, my body is sore and wounded. In the church meeting I came back to Jesus. I know He has forgiven me. But I still need someone whose words can heal me."

"Tell me what is troubling you," Ngolo urged.

Paul Lamba related his story step by step: initial events which led him to compromise with the revolution, the suffering and deprivation of him and his people in the forest which was slowly leading them toward death, his secret arrangements to renounce the rebel authority and defect to military forces, his disguising plans by telling a lie, and their final liberation.

"While I know that Jesus has restored me," Lamba continued, "there are still questions which perplex me. If God really loves us, explain to me; how can He allow us to be caught in this kind of suffering? Why does He watch silently while His children die? If a person tells a lie in order to bring such suffering to an end, has he sinned? The path I chose to follow helped bring a man to his death. Do I carry responsibility for him? Pastor, if you can answer these questions, my pain will be finished."

Pastor Ngolo thoughtfully weighed the questions of the troubled man and then respectfully addressed him.

"Father Paul, when a man's house burns down, there is no way that he can understand everything about it while his eyes still smart from its smoke. Later he will understand some things about it better. Also, he may come to see that it is not important that he understand everything. You have just passed through the fire. How can you expect to comprehend every-

287

thing? Later you may come to understand some things better. But we must remember that God has not chosen to give us sight to understand everything."

Paul Lamba sat motionless listening intently. Pastor Ngolo continued.

"Though we do not understand everything, the Bible teaches us some things clearly. One thing is that God loves us. The death of His Son on the cross for us should dispel all doubts of people about that forever. Another thing the Bible teaches clearly is this: God cannot compel men to pursue a course which they do not choose to follow. When they follow wrong paths, He grieves. When they decided to kill His Son, did He stop them? What they did caused Him such pain that He covered His eyes to not see it. If He allowed evil men to cause His own Son to suffer and die, why would He not allow us to suffer and die?"

It seemed the stress lines on Lamba's face were beginning to relax. The pastor resumed his counsel.

"God is not happy to watch His child suffer. He is distressed. But He does not allow the suffering of His child to be wasted like something discarded into a garbage pit. God makes use of that suffering. Look how He used the suffering of His Son! That suffering became a sufficient price to redeem everything He had created! The Bible teaches that God glorified Jesus and made Him perfect by means of the things which He suffered. If we who follow Him are to be His bride, how can we be suitable for Him if we have never known suffering? How could we be happy living with Him forever if we are unlike Him? So when suffering catches us, God uses it to prepare us so that when the time comes, we will feel good to sit with Jesus."

Slowly the man's face began to light with understanding.

"The Book of God tells us what is right and what is wrong," the pastor continued. "It says that lying is wrong. We are Christians. We follow the footsteps of Jesus. When a hunter pursues an animal, sometimes its tracks are difficult to see. Sometimes the tracks disappear and the hunter strays from side to side for a while until he finds them again. Does his straying mean that he is a poor hunter? No. But what would we say if a hunter turns around to study the line of tracks his own feet have made? In the same way, a Christian should not carry a burden of sorrow for tracks he has made. His work is to discern and follow the tracks of Jesus. Inasmuch as God has not given us sight to understand everything, He knows that times will come when we stray. If we lose sight of the trail, that does not mean we are poor Christians. God provides for our weakness. He promises us all the grace we need to cover the sinning we do in our blindness. When we fail, He asks us to accept His forgiveness and to keep on following Him."

Pastor Paul Lamba was beaming now.

"My brother, your words are medicine for my soul," he said. "They heal me. They strengthen me. I glorify God that you and the young men came to search us out. If you had not come, what would I have done?"

The man paused and suddenly became somber as if he had recalled something.

"What else is troubling you?" Ngolo asked.

"When we were in the forest I received a letter from James Ilunga. He was calling me to come join him. Have you heard news about him?"

Pastor Ngolo hesitated and fingered his Bible nervously.

"That is a matter which causes me great sadness," he replied. "James Ilunga and his wife were living with the rebels in a valley stronghold. James was suffering from rheumatism. When soldiers came, he was not able to flee. They found him in his house. They refused to believe that he was a pastor. They killed him. Later soldiers saw women in a manioc field. They called for them to surrender. The wife of Ilunga was among them. She and another woman turned and fled. The soldiers shot them."

Lamba gaped at the pastor, then shook his head in dismay.

"God has shown you mercy," Ngolo continued. "He still has work for you to do. Let's pray together. Then I will begin speaking with the next person."

Pastor Ngolo and the theological students counseled with people the rest of Sunday, all day

Monday, and finished about Tuesday noon. For another week they ministered to refugees in surrounding villages. Then about midafternoon one day a large truck arrived. It had distributed relief supplies and had picked up other student teams ministering in the region. Now it had come to pick up the Kende team before returning home. Pastor David Ngolo tossed his baggage into the rear of the bed and climbed into the right side of the cab. The driver took his place behind the wheel and started the motor. The truck lurched and they were on their way.

All that could be heard now was the monotonous roar of the motor. It was a fitting time for reflection. These had been momentous days. Ngolo rejoiced at what he and his friends had witnessed. About five hundred persons had sought counsel and had surrendered themselves to the Lord. Over half of them were youth who had been partisans in the revolution. They had confessed a startling variety of misdeeds. Over fifty of them sought pardon for taking human life. One repentant young man expressed the sentiments of them all when he said, "We all of us coveted a leopard's pelt; when we got it, it turned into worms."

Young Kimbody had recognized three men among the defiant rebels being detained for execution. He gained permission to talk with them, led them to repent of their sins, and then persuaded the military commander to liberate

291

them. Several soldiers had come seeking to give themselves to Christ. The theological students had distributed three truckloads of relief supplies to all who were in need. That was the work of the Kende team alone.

These had been extremely difficult days for the church in the Kwilu. People had made mistakes. But they also had demonstrated remarkable heroism. Pastor David recalled such incidents in the experiences of Paul Lamba, James Ilunga, Stephen Kimeya, Kimeya's father Kapala, and many others. He recalled previous hazardous trips he and students had made to rescue believers. It was not easy to see at this time what good was coming out of these troubled times. But one thing was clear. The mortar which bound the church together and enabled it to survive was the power of Christ in the hearts of His people which compelled them to love one another.

Pearls of rain began to thump the windshield. It was that time of year. Showers had begun to come regularly now, almost every afternoon. The experienced pastor watched between swipes of the windshield wiper as huge drops pummeled the green grass and washed the face of the earth again. The Spirit of the Lord was like that. He could be relied upon to do His work. He washes away the unhappy memories of pain and confusion and failure. He penetrates deeply. He makes seeds forsake their rotting carcasses. He causes hidden stirrings of strength which always bring forth the fresh green shoots of new life again.

"Thank you, my Lord," Ngolo whispered. "You continue the work of establishing Your church; and truly, the gates of hell cannot overcome it."

The employees of G.K. Hall hope you have enjoyed this Large Print book. All our Large Print titles are designed for easy reading, and all our books are made to last. Other G.K. Hall books are available at your library, through selected bookstores, or directly from us.

For information about titles, please call:

(800) 257-5157

To share your comments, please write:

Publisher
G.K. Hall & Co.
P.O. Box 159
Thorndike, ME 04986